"Jesse Ball is a writer of formal mysteriousness and neon moral clarity. . . . His language is spare, strange, and evocative. . . . His themes are human savagery, often state-sanctioned, and human kindness, a thin thread of resistance. . . . The final section [of *The Divers' Game*] is breathtaking." —*The New Yorker*

"A book that contemplates, with the gravity and grace it deserves, a world beyond the point of no return. . . . Stunning. . . . The book's final section, in which a woman confronts the violence within herself, is one of the more beautiful things I've ever read." —*The Paris Review*

"It's hard to read a book like *The Divers' Game*—in which an unnamed nation receives an influx of refugees and abandons the notion of human fellow feeling—and not immediately think of the present moment. . . . [An] interlocking puzzle box of a novel, artful and often inscrutable. . . . The society in *The Divers' Game* uses rituals like festivals and games to paper over its own violence. They merely reveal how untenable that violence is." —*The New York Times Book Review*

"Jesse Ball (*Census*) levels a steely gaze at the very concept of humanity in this three-part novel that introduces the lower-class 'quads' and the rich 'pats,' who treat those below them with impunity. When a group of pats conceals the grisly fate of a young quad girl behind an elaborate festival, you may start to wonder just how different this dystopian world is from our own." —*The Washington Post*

"Affecting . . . uncomfortably familiar. . . . [*The Divers' Game*] should certainly make you question what kind of world we are preparing for the generations to come."   —*amNewYork*

"Radical. . . . If they don't teach Ball's work in college by now, they should. . . . Readers who appreciate Ball's keen, melancholic, and often sadly satirical view of human society will likely appreciate this timely assessment of where division might take us and how it affects the generations that come after us."
   —*Kirkus Reviews*

"Mesmerizing . . . Ball (*Census*) delivers a strident condemnation of inequality in an imagined nation. . . . The novel's depiction of life in this dystopian world is eerie and suffused with symbolic weight."   —*Publishers Weekly*

"Ball (*Census*, 2018), a writer of exceptional and pensive imagination, adds another trenchant fable to his distinctively disquieting oeuvre. . . . One hears the beat of *Animal Farm*. . . . Writing with blood-freezing sparseness, Ball illuminates this calamitously immoral place. . . . Distressingly mirrors aspects of our own [world]."   —*Booklist*

THE DIVERS' GAME

THE DIVERS' GAME

A NOVEL

JESSE BALL

ecco

An Imprint of HarperCollins*Publishers*

HarperCollins books may be purchased for educational, business, or sales promotional use. For information, please email the Special Markets Department at SPsales@harpercollins.com.

Ecco® and HarperCollins® are trademarks of HarperCollins Publishers.

A hardcover edition of this book was published in 2019 by Ecco, an imprint of HarperCollins Publishers.

FIRST ECCO PAPERBACK EDITION PUBLISHED 2020

Designed by Renata De Oliveira

Library of Congress Cataloging-in-Publication Data

Names: Ball, Jesse, 1978- author.
Title: The divers' game : a novel / Jesse Ball.
Description: New York : Ecco, 2019.
Identifiers: LCCN 2018051083 | ISBN 9780062676108
Classification: LCC PS3602.A596 D58 2019 | DDC 813/.6—
    dc23 LC record available at https://lccn.loc.gov/2018051083

ISBN 978-0-06-267612-2 (pbk.)

20 21 22 23 24   LSC   10 9 8 7 6 5 4 3 2 1

CONTENTS

THE DIVERS'
GAME

Ogias' Day

*I heard a song once:
at the moment of my despair someone
was singing on the other side of the
fence, a young voice, a voice that
could hardly have known what it was
singing, what the words meant, or
who they were meant for.*

1

Lethe! If we look for her, if we run up the stairs, cast open her door, and look in her bed, she is not there. If we dash down the steps, turn a corner, pass her befuddled father (who cannot see us), and go to the little table that she loves so well, the one by the window, she is not there! She is not there! A plate and some crumbs, an empty glass. Out we go into the street, and up ahead—can it be?—we see her, beneath linden trees, swaying as a child does, because the morning sways, because when it is the morning, isn't everything swaying? It is only the old who are stiff, who can no longer feel the world's slight breath.

Lethe! She is looking at her feet as she walks, watching them—how unpredictable they are, are they hers?—and thinking—what will she do today? Her feet move beneath, and we with them, and suddenly we have reached the train. Nimbly up the steps she goes, the train doors open, and there is a place for her, between two men who stare straight ahead, as if into nothing. They are not alone. The train is full of such as they. Lethe takes her place among them. She looks straight ahead, but her mind is humming. This is a trip she takes each morning, and meanwhile, always meanwhile, she is elsewhere.

The doors close, the train shoves forward, and over the loudspeaker comes a voice she has heard a thousand times. Instinctively, she grasps the gray rubber device on her belt and straightens up. She stares ahead, chin up, almost proudly. A deep and reassuring voice, the ever familiar voice, one she has heard her whole life, it shudders the speakers and everyone in the car chants softly:

A citizen
For the life of him
Or her or he or she
That keeps a mask
On the belt or arm
Need never fear the streets.
If trouble comes
Like quad scum—
Your mask put on!
Your mask put on!

The gas shall flow
A cloud to grow
And lay them low
The lowest at our feet.

A chorus of horns plays, and the car is quiet again. It travels on, ever forward. That is the direction of society: forward. All those who try to send it back are ground beneath the wheels. Hasn't it always been so?

At every station, the joyful chorus peals. When you are so used to saying something—isn't it a kind of gladness to let it roll unexamined from your lips? They stood in that tincture, a thin gladness to be sure—you could never touch it, or really feel it, until the train doors opened at the center exchange, and out the passengers poured, so many—you would never think the train could hold so many. They were not in wild colors, these citizens, although of course they wore the latest fashions. And each, to the last, bore a finely made mask upon the hip. Have you ever seen so many gas masks in one place? And every one nicely worn from use, every one the tool of an expert. It was a kind of modern-day Sparta, wouldn't you say that? Wouldn't you agree?

And today, it was the day before Ogias' Day. There hadn't been an Ogias' Day, not for fifty years. So no one knew how it would go.

LETHE MANAGED HER WAY DOWN THE STAIRS FROM THE platform, and ducked under a rail to take a shortcut along a green bank to a side street that ran out hurriedly from the rail exchange. This was the way to her school, for she was grown now, sixteen or seventeen, and could take her place at a college, where she would be taught everything a person might want to know, everything about anything. Lethe was the kind of clever that doesn't say much. She was liked and praised and left alone. Her future was assured. But today she was late to school, only just late, and ran in the front door through a sort of absence—the throng had passed through three moments before. She could almost feel them there, a wild mass of arms and legs, of shoving and nearness. One, two, three—and then she!

Into the classroom, and she sought for Lois. In her mind in the door she saw Lois, imagined her in some chair, with a free space beside her. Then, into the lecture hall, and Lois was there, just as she had seen it, just as Lois always was, beckoning with a thin arm, an arm that looked almost precisely like Lethe's. I could not tell them apart, though they were not sisters. Have you ever met someone and felt they were some reflection of you? Have you felt reflected? Lethe and Lois sat and held hands beneath the desks, identical in gray skirts and dry yellow sweaters, bare at the shoulder. The light at the podium flickered on, and their lecturer, Mandred, was there. His old eyes raked the room, and he smiled slightly.

And shall we begin?

YOU ALL REMEMBER WE WERE SPEAKING LAST WEEK about the circumstances that led to the transformation of our society. The famous influx of refugees—so many they could not help but change us. We were forced by them to change. Everyone remembers the lesson? How did we change?

That's right, the Firstmost Proposal. This was the subject of our test last week. Can someone tell me the substance of the Firstmost Proposal? You?

That's wrong. It's not entirely right, and what we say is, what is entirely right is right, everything else is wrong. The Firstmost Proposal, I remind you, was made by Eavan Garing. A minor elected official at the time, he would later be chancellor. He said, we can welcome them, as long as we can tell them apart. *As long as we can tell them apart.* Many of them, wherever they were from, they had red hats, a kind of long knit hat, a red hat, no one remembers why, and so Garing said, *This will be their symbol.* We'll tattoo the red hat on their cheeks, and then we'll know who is who. Then we can welcome them.

Did this work?

Yes, it worked, the refugees were admitted, and they were told apart. What else did it mean? What else did the red hat mean?

That's right: *They shall have red hats so you may know them, and they shall therefore have no legal standing as persons.* It was the kindest thing that could be done, to admit them, because they had nowhere to go, but they were different than we are, and that fact couldn't be forgotten.

So then they were among us, and bore their red hats, but there was trouble. Who remembers what the trouble was?

Yes, they had no safety; they were not persons, anything could be done to them. Certain low elements, citizens to be sure, but low elements, well, they were taking advantage. It was causing trouble. It wasn't any good to see, especially not within the nation. And of course this made others become partisan. Some were actually sympathetic to the newcomers. Groups were organized, a kind of vigilante militia, to protect them, to protect the refugees from other citizens. Do you recall the names of any of them? This was material from a previous class. Someone should know it.

That's right, Lambert Ma. He was among the first. He murdered several citizens before he was arrested and executed. There was a good deal of blood shed, the blood of full citizens, as well as a great deal of attrition among the refugee group. Their population declined measurably at this time. But it did not go away.

What happened then?

Yes, the government suppressed these partisans, in effect supporting which position?

That anything could be done to those without rights. There is a philosophical position that came into vogue, it is what we call in philosophy an awakening, a large-scale shift in belief: that things done to those beneath are not properly violence. It was a new definition of violence, and helped to create a vibrant morality, one that infuses our nation to this day. Our morality is *what we do*. Do you all understand that? But if what we do ceases to be violence, let us say it is the same, but it is no longer violence: then we are not violent; we are no longer doers of violence.

Nonetheless we have hearts, we are a good and fair society. It was clear the refugees could not simply live amongst us without trouble. So someone thought of the first quad, the very first quadrant. The government at that time surveyed areas that they called quadrants, outside of each city, and within the quadrants, these who had no rights, the refugees—how did it go? Did they have rights? It was a new kind of land, one that had never existed before, a new designation. Did they have rights there?

No, that's correct, they did not gain rights within their quadrants, no, the quadrants were surrounded by walls, as they are today, with guards, to see that there could be no organized revolt. But the guards don't keep anyone in place. Anyone can pass in and out, as you know, but within the walls, and here is the point—this is why there was suddenly safety, a kind of safety: within those walls, no one had any rights, not even a citizen. This was deemed precivilized space.

And so those with the red hats, they have come to be known, vulgarly, as *quads*. And they may come out and take jobs in the nation, but they may remain within their quadrants if they like. The government provides them with food and clothing there, so they need not even work. And we as citizens, we who compose the nation, we may go where we like, even into the quads, but if something were to happen to us in a quadrant, what would it mean? If I went into a quad and someone murdered me, what would it mean?

That's right—it would mean nothing. It would have happened within precivilized space. There is no rule of law there. Of course, the guards can go in and effect searches, seizures, but that is a different matter, a military matter. In any case, let me ask you, how is this order preserved— how do the citizens stay safe? Why is it that we can master the quads when they come out into the nation, however many they are, whatever their intentions? What is our tool? What is it?

He held up his mask, the mask that hung on his belt. It was an old-style mask, the one that is often shown on posters.

Yes, yes, the gas. That was also Garing's idea. Four colors of gas, each with a use, and the citizens protected, always protected from the gas. You have all lived your whole life in the comfort of the gas—with the freedom it affords you. You have walked down avenues beside running gas lines, every ten feet a junction head posted. You have been raised with the drills: don the mask, run to the pavement marked K. You know the beautiful feeling of safety. You understand the gas. Still, it was not so simple at first. There were many who stood against it.

Today though we are speaking not about the Firstmost Proposal, not about the gas, but about the Secondmost Proposal. Does anyone know it?

LETHE KNEW WHAT THE FIRSTMOST PROPOSAL WAS.
She knew what the gas was, even some of its chemistry. Her father was a scientist. She knew the Secondmost Proposal, the basic history of the nation. But Lois beside her knew none of it. They had been raised rather differently. And so whereas Lois leaned forward, eager to hear what the Secondmost Proposal was, Lethe tapped an ankle nervously against the chair and drew whirligig circles on a sheet of paper. None were perfect. She thought about the thick rim of the wood desk and pressed her thumb against it. There was a sharp edge, and she found it, and played with it, pressing her arm there, a pressure just before she would be cut. Have you played this game as a child? Do you play it still? To test every sensation of the body? Lethe pressed and gritted her teeth.

Lois on the other hand watched Mandred, and her expression was soft, lunar—distant but welcoming. She enjoyed her classes and was good at them but had never known a thing beforehand, the way Lethe did. Perhaps it could be said she was better than Lethe at learning things she didn't know.

What was he saying?

Mandred was saying that it had once been true that criminals were sent to places called prisons. Prison, how would that be spelled? One s or two? Lois perked up her ears.

The professor droned on:

The Secondmost Proposal, yes, well, it did not immediately follow the first; it was years later, but it was the Secondmost because it was also made by Garing. He realized that the quads were working so well, we might expand them. Why should we send criminals, by the thousand and million, to penitentiaries, prisons, and jails when we could simply join them to the quad population? And so it was done. This problem that had troubled the nation for hundreds of years, done away with in a moment. The prisons were disbanded. Every prisoner was branded with the red hat, and every prisoner had the right thumb taken, so that the difference would be obvious, always obvious. For consistency, those in the quads also had to have their thumbs taken. This was the cause of a great deal of unrest, but of course it was easily suppressed. They cannot stand against the gas.

Mandred pressed a button on the podium, and a screen rolled down behind him.

Now we will watch the thumb-taking procedure—one that goes on even now, in this very city.

He went and sat in the first row, and the light on the podium dimmed to nothing. Numbers appeared on the screen, counting down, and an image came, of a facility from above, a long, narrow black building, with a track outside, like a fairground. In the lines of tracks stood thousands of people. It was a film of that first day, and no one in that line knew what was going to happen. But everyone in the classroom knew. There was an expectation, like a spasm of joy. How much we like to be distinguished from those who are not our equals.

Meanwhile, Lethe had left the class. She went out and sat by a tree. The day wasn't cold at all; it was warm, and the sun was mocking the clouds, going in and out of them. The shadows on the ground moved this way and that, as if in response. A boy joined her there. She recognized him from somewhere, a long athletic type with a thin mouth. What was his name? Gerard?

Hey Lethe.

She nodded.

You in Mandred's.

She nodded.

He's a drunk, did you know that?

Shook her head.

Yeah, his wife died last year. Since then (the boy mimed a person with a bottle).

Why did she die?

Dunno.

They sat there for a few minutes, and trucks came and went on the avenue by the school.

Gerard stood up.

I think, I think it was. Someone told me she gassed herself. She didn't want to live, and when Mandred found her, all he could do was hit the bottle from then on. He's a drunk.

Gerard laughed.

Well, bye.

He went inside, and Lethe sat a little longer. She thought about what it would mean to feel the gas, and shivered. She imagined it wouldn't feel like anything at all, and she was right, partly. She thought about being alone in a room and feeling that extinguishing wildness that wants to end life. People are coming to help you, but they are on the stair, they are even behind the door, but there is not time to open it, for you have opened the canister, you have breathed the gas—like a wing's flap your life has extended and elapsed, and it cannot be taken back.

INSIDE, LOIS WAS JOINED BY LETHE. THE FILM WAS proceeding at the minimum speed of illusion. They held hands again, and watched. Who could say what it was like to watch such a film? The girls' eyes were full of it—the surface of the eyes received it all, admitted it all: a menagerie of trembling light as men in white uniforms—they looked like dairy workers or men at the butcher's counter—caught and held down all kinds of people, every kind of person, men, women, boys, girls, people of every color, shape, size. The thumb-taking room seemed very clean and bare. It was a kind of theater. There was always one person to be held down, and many people to do it, so it worked out as it should, even though every single person resisted. It was almost comical. A door would pop open. The next one would come into the room, would stiffen, try to raise their arms, then their arms would be taken, they would break free, be grabbed again, forced down into something like a stocks, and then there was no more resistance. There was no sound, so if there was shrieking, it is lost to history. The film was long, and they watched it all, watched thumb after thumb be taken, watched cheek after cheek be branded. When there were farms, it was like this—the slaughter of the animals. They would be led to slaughter. But here no one was slaughtered, just changed a little. There was one boy in particular. Lois saw him and felt he looked like her brother. She didn't have a brother, but she'd always wanted one, and here in the film, here he was. She watched them hold him down and take his thumb. It was a slender, dark thumb and could easily have been hers. His face was pressed down by the branding iron, and it happened, a strange thing happened—many of those who were branded, the expression of their pain was a kind of grin. Why was that? Why were they all grinning in this horrible way? She tried it on her face, the same grin, and saw that Lethe beside her, she was grinning too.

The film was at its conclusion, and a gray blackness flickered where it had been.

YOU MUST FEEL, SAID MANDRED, RISING, WHETHER you do or not, you must try to feel that this work is a good work, however hard it is to do. You never want to be the sort of person who flinches from the work that is hard. Even if someone else does it for you, you must realize how hard it is, and how beautiful it is, how right, that it is done, and done well.

We are speaking of a pile of thumbs that could fill a stadium. They did not get there by themselves. That's why I wanted you to see this. Tomorrow we will have a test on the Secondmost Proposal. You will read the assigned material, and I will ask you, in the test, to quote parts at length, so be prepared. That is all for now. Thank you.

The lights came on, and suddenly everyone could see one another. They had all seen this grisly sight, all felt separated, alone in the face of it, but then with the lights on, they could see one another, familiarly, happily. Although they were not, it was almost as though they rubbed against one another all at once like cats, a happiness born from sameness, and in that spirit they poured out of the lecture hall.

But three remained. One below the podium, two in the seats above.

Quietly: What is it?

I want to ask him something, said Lois.

MANDRED WAS PUTTING PAPERS INTO A LEATHER valise at the bottom of the concavity. They went down to him, in a darting procession of legs.

When they came opposite, they lifted themselves backward onto the carpeted stage and sat feet dangling. The young are so quick, so agile! Their limbs so strong! Now it was they who watched him.

And then Lois was speaking, she was asking her question:

Why was it always the right thumb? You would think that they would want to take the dominant thumb, but that isn't always the same, is it?

Lethe peered at Lois, and Mandred nodded.

This is a good question—I don't have time to answer it now, but . . .

He paused in thought. No, no. But then he reconsidered.

I am going later on a special day trip. My assistant is sick. If you want to come along, you could act as my assistant. We'd have more time to talk about this, this thumb conjecture. It's an hour's train ride. What is your name again?

Lois.

How would that be?

Lois looked at Lethe. Lethe looked at Lois.

I think so. Can Lethe come too?

Mandred looked the two of them over, as if regretting his proposal, but the cloud passed and he smiled suddenly. What did he smile at?

Yes, he said, Lethe can come. Lethe. It's a strange name.

Lethe looked confused.

When would we be back?

Not late, not too late.

She's just asking that because she's dutiful. She's always home for her parents, like clockwork, aren't you?

Shut up.

It won't be late. Don't worry about that.

He went up the steps and out. At the door he turned off the lights and paused.

You didn't even ask me where we are going, Lethe, Lois.

They stared at his outline against the light.

We are going to a zoo, a real zoo. I'll leave at three from the front entrance.

THE GIRLS WERE IN CONSTERNATION. A ZOO. NEITHER had ever been to such a place. Zoos were like barge trips, and mountain retreats, they were for party functionaries, high officials, the very wealthy. Regular people did not get to go to the zoo.

Lethe could hardly believe it.

There's no zoo. The old man just wants to strangle you in some back corridor.

Awful, don't say it.

I think he does.

He won't.

You should let him.

You should, you can be his assistant.

No, you. You're the one he asked.

The two girls sat in the dark, joking and saying this or that, touching each other lightly on the face or arm. None of it meant anything, but the whole of it was of course as meaningful as a thing could be. To be alongside another person, and somehow in them, in their eyes and mind, to feel what they feel, and have what you feel be felt? And all in a soft darkness, a film just finished, the freedom of free hours beckoning. And ahead—a zoo!

THEY HAD GONE DOWN TO EAT SOMETHING BY THE fountain. They sat on the edge and said things to each other. People walked by in the midst of drab lives, not even conscious that the moment passing was *that* moment. Likewise Lethe and Lois were elsewhere—they were in the next day, speaking rapidly, almost glowing.

Ogias' Day had been announced not yesterday and not the day before that but the day before that. Lois said the moment she heard, she had gotten herself a light-blue dress with blue boots and a burned-red rain cover. When she described her clothing, it was almost as if it appeared in the air before them, rotating in a kind of glory. How delightful!

I will take my Salman b3 because it's the same blue, she said. It was my mother's idea. She said Ogias' Day has a traditional blue tint. In the festive materials, blue, so the b3 will be perfect. I guess I prefer the Gotch 2 (here she patted the mustard-yellow mask at her waist), but the b3 is so nice.

Lethe blushed slightly at this—she had only one mask, not several like Lois.

I like that one. I tried it at the store. It is quite narrow.

Well, my face is narrow, like a shrew.

They both laughed.

I don't even know what a shrew looks like.

Me neither.

Maybe we'll see one at the zoo!

A man walking past turned. He stared at them a moment too long. Lois peered at him and waved him over.

What is it, miss?

He was old, and wore a worker's coveralls. He seemed to instinctively flinch.

She said something. He couldn't hear, and she waved him closer. He couldn't hear again, and she waved him closer. He hesitated, but came and was standing there practically in between them.

I'm sorry, he said. Can I?

Could you go fuck yourself.

Lethe burst out laughing, but Lois kept a straight face, staring right at the guy.

Go fuck yourself, she repeated. And don't look at us.

She's just like that, said Lethe. Don't worry. It isn't about you.

Unless it is, said Lois. Maybe it is about you.

He shook a bit and hurried away. They both laughed some more and watched him go.

Would you ever gas somebody?

What? asked Lethe.

Would you gas somebody, if you had to?

Of course. Wouldn't you?

I definitely would if I had to—I guess what I mean then is, what if you didn't have to? What if you just wanted to? Would you do it? Do you ever think about gassing someone?

You know Mandred's wife gassed herself. She tugged off the end of a canister and breathed it all in. That's what some guy told me.

Wait, she's dead?

Yeah—last year. Same guy said that's why Mandred's a drunk.

Is he a drunk?

I don't know.

Why would she do that?

I guess there are a lot of reasons.

Yeah. Huh. What are you going in tomorrow?

I think that Litnas jacket with the pants.

Didn't I make fun of you the last time you wore that?

You promised you wouldn't again.

You're only going to wear it because what's his name came to talk to you because the top is so—

Shut up, it isn't. What was his name? He was from—

Do you want to come by my house in the morning and we can go together?

Sure.

A man came up and offered to sell them replacement filters for their masks. They declined. He went on to the next group, farther along the fountain, and gave the same speech, got the same reply.

I'd never trust those, said Lethe. Who knows where they came from?

Hey, said Lois. From the lecture. I don't get what he said about safety. Why is it safer for the niners in Baseltown or Row House? Isn't it dangerous in there? Everyone talks about the horrible things that happen. My mom said she's never been in a quad and she would never go. When my father started in about his visit to a quad, she made him stop. If it's so bad, why do they like it in there?

Well, it's safer for us out here, obviously. But in there—it's safer for them because no one can gas them. Except the guards. Out here anything that happens to them is fine. They have to be on their toes—all the time. You know that.

Lois nodded.

Like that poor fuck just now. I never want to get old.

A truck went by with a loudspeaker on the back. It blared the gas creed, and everyone stood to attention. No bird looked down upon the scene, however, because there were no birds left to perch on anything, no birds left to look down on anything. The girls we've passed the morning with had never seen a bird, or any other animal for that matter. It was a new world.

The girls' behavior—does it seem cruel? You have to understand, it isn't cruel so much as natural. What is natural must be respected, must be wallowed in. Isn't it so?

Why should they bother to care about someone so inferior? It makes perfect sense that service of every kind should be given by those who can provide it. Those who are ridiculous bear ridicule. Those who are beneath notice are not noticed, and those who are elect are raised up.

As much as we like to think there can be fairness, it is really a foolish idea, one we ought to have done away with long ago. Instead of fairness there is just order and its consequences.

Humans of the past were often hobbled when they saw other humans and felt themselves like to them. Was this not the cause of so many wars, a series of wars leading up to a final, enormous war that might have ruined everything?

We are not alike! We are only alike to those who we are like to, to those who are known, certainly known, to be the same as we. This is proven in the course of time.

AND IN FACT ON THE FOUNTAIN WHERE THE GIRLS HAD sat, there was raised lettering, a scroll in the hands of a girl, half-fish, half-human. Do you know what it said? It was one of the creeds, one of the most important creeds, the creed of the elect. The girls had probably never looked into the fountain and seen it, but the creed they felt in their hearts.

A world of tiers—
Know your place upon it
By looking down.

Be strong!

HE CAME ALONG THE HALL AND SAW THEM STANDING
there, each the other's shadow, leaning provocatively on
the window casement. His eyes lingered on them. Of
course!—those girls—they were to come with him. A good
thing he'd come down that hall and not another. He'd
forgotten their names. What were they? One was . . . One
was . . . It was as if he swam in a cloud, surfacing to
clarity and diving again. He'd been lying on his back on
the floor of his office for the last hour. What were their
names?

They were saying something, they were greeting him.

Girls. I think you'll find this trip worth your while. The
zoo director is an old friend. He is proofreading a book that
I wrote.

About what?

What's that?

Lethe wants to know what the book is about.

It is a comparison of lives. Statesmen from the New Ep-
och, and statesmen from the old, the lives told so that they
frame one another.

The girls said they were unlikely to read a book like that.

He snorted.

Well, it isn't for you, not unless you want to read it, and then of course you could, if you found it.

Lethe shook her head.

I won't read it unless you put some women in there.

Oh, I see, he said. Confusion in the ranks. . . . You see, *statesmen* includes women. There are women in the book, don't worry.

They argued about whether statesmen includes women. The girls did not believe it.

At the station they were to board a train for the outer circuit of the city, which lay beyond a kind of ringed park area. The Center was where people lived, there and in the First and Second district. Beyond that was the ring of parkland, and then the industrial areas. There was also, of course, the quad.

They were looking at a map. Everything on the map was drawn smaller than its actual size, of course, because it was a map and that's how maps work, but the quad was drawn even smaller than anything else. People didn't like to look at it.

Will we see Gall Roads from the train?

It's behind a series of berms. But we'll pass it.

He ran his finger along the route that they would take.

ON THE TRAIN THEY SAT IN A BOX WITH TWO OPPOSING benches. The girls occupied one, he the other. Lethe whispered in Lois's ear, something about the stench of liquor. It was all too much—they were giddy. Anyone would be. They leaned into each other and breathed and breathed.

The ever familiar voice came, and they stood and said the gas creed and sat again.

When the train lurched, Lethe's bag fell over and a book slid out. The old man picked it up. He coughed.

Tradition and Culture of Row House. A very famous and controversial book. Which of you is reading it?

Lethe raised a finger.

And what do you think?

Lethe said something, but the train drowned her out.

Mandred squinted.

She said nothing is simple—even the quads. So it makes sense that they would have . . . what was it?

Inner lives.

Inner lives.

Ah. Inner lives.

He said the words with a scowl in his mouth.

Well, there are differing opinions about this book. Some people think it is largely fantasy. You see—when a person, in this case an anthropologist, goes to study people, the people are affected by the fact that they are being studied.

Lethe rolled her eyes.

The point is, he continued, the human mind seeks out patterns, and even creates them, even creates them from chaos. It finds patterns where there are none. Row House was a terrible slum, is a terrible slum, has always been a terrible slum. For a long time it was thought of as the worst of the quads.

But she was so brave to go in there. Lethe told me about what she did, going in there by herself, and staying in there for days at a time. The people even protected her while she wrote it. She won them over.

And do you know what happened to her?

The two girls shook their heads.

She was raped and killed in Solston. Not in Row House but in Solston. A man just grabbed her in the street, and no one helped. No one knew her there. It went on for an hour. They say the guards saw it and didn't help either, because they knew who she was. The guards didn't come out well in her book, so they felt she was their enemy. There was an opinion, well, some people thought she got what was coming to her. Some people even said she might have been a quad that somehow managed to escape the branding and thumb taking. Every now and then it happens. They're crafty.

There is a part, Lethe said, where there's a funeral. The quads think there's another life after this one. They think it matters what you do in this life because to get to the next one you need to do certain things.

The old man laughed.

Yes, we all used to think that. Everyone. It's hard to believe, isn't it?

Can you answer my question now?

Mandred tried to remember what the question had been. He looked at his hands in his lap, and at the cover of the book he was holding. It didn't come to him. His embarrassment was plain.

Lethe nudged Lois.

It was about the thumb taking. Why not take the dominant thumb?

Oh, yes, the thumb taking. A very good question. In fact, they do take the dominant thumb now. But at the start they didn't have the time to test for hand dominance. The essence of this question is of interest. That essence is: What is the heart of the enterprise? Is it to make the quad less efficient, to render him weaker and less competent? Is it merely an echo of the ancestral law: to cut off the hand of a thief? Is it a quick cataloguing gesture, that of a librarian, to clip off the same corner of every page? Which do you think?

Lethe whispered to Lois.

She thought it was the last one, cataloguing, so it's odd they alter which thumb. How many lefties are there anyway?

I have always thought it was inconsistent. It would be better if they just took all right thumbs, as they did at the start. For instance, it means that when a guard is inspecting a person, at a random checkpoint, for instance, he must check both thumbs to see if they are prosthetic, rather than merely one. This in effect doubles his workload.

I met a guard once, said Lois.

I think we have all seen them, haven't we?

I mean socially. He came to my parents' house. He was a regular citizen, not a bottom-grader like most of them. For some reason he decided to join up. I guess anyone can.

She flashed a look at Lethe.

He was kind of good-looking. But I was just nine then. I remember he picked me up and twirled me around in the air and my heart beat so fast. I could feel him holding me there at my waist for days.

Well, they aren't all like that.

Lethe looked out the window. There was a waterway off to the left, a thin gray-blue line, and alongside it a series of low dwellings, each in perfect order. The landscape was devoid of people. Why is it that wherever we go when we look for people we can find no one? Where is everyone? Where have they gone?

THE TRAIN STOPPED AT THE NEXT STATION, AND A DOOR opened. A large man entered their compartment and sat down in the box opposite theirs. He was looking at a newssheet. He noticed them staring and turned, and the raw red brand on his cheek stuck out.

Mandred looked at the girls, then at the man. He stood up and went over and spoke to him. What he said was too quiet to hear, but the man got up and left the car.

What did you say to him?

He should know better. What is he doing, sitting right there? Sometimes I think the Forthright Doctrine has gone too far. Sure they should feel like people, but they aren't people, at least not when real people are around.

What did you say?

Mandred snorted.

I told him if he didn't get out right then, that would be it for him. Just like that. I know you think it's harsh, but it's the only way. You have to speak like that. The niners are children, essentially. They don't progress beyond a certain point. They don't understand abstract things.

Well, I'm glad he's gone, said Lois. He was awfully big. I'd hate to be alone with him.

What would you have done if he hadn't left?

Mandred seemed confused by the question. He sat down.

The fact of disposal. It's an interesting subject. When the prisoners were first released, gassings were common. Before that, those in prison who were to be executed had to go through an enormous rigmarole. It was no easy thing to handle an execution. Yet when the prisoners became quads, when they essentially went on to continue their bad behavior in the midst of life, regular citizens started doing what needed doing, started the business of disposal for themselves. That is to say, these new quads who had been criminals were often simply gassed the first wrong they did. It happened that a housewife at a tram station would pull a lever or pop a canister, settle her mask on her face, and lay down two or three of them at once. A child might do it, just the same. He'd feel afraid when a few of them joined him in some alley he was walking down, and the end of his canister would pop—and that would be that.

Of course, the different gases helped to make people feel more comfortable with using them. The yellow killing gas, the green incapacitating gas, the red gas that confuses, the brown gas that sickens, the slow killer.

Which do you have? Lethe asked.

Mandred showed her the brown lid of his canister.

I like the color of the yellow, said Lois. We both have that. Don't we?

They lifted their sweaters to show the canisters at their waists, both mud yellow. Mandred looked on.

Lethe laughed. She whispered something, but it was hard to hear because the wheels of the train were rattling.

The old man stood and went to the bathroom compartment. It was a brief area, tucked behind a door. The door shut with a loud snap, and he was alone. He leaned against the wall heavily and pulled a pint from his coat pocket. He raised it, raised it again.

IF WE LEAVE HIM THERE AND GO BACK ALONG THE CAR, we see the girls from behind, we see the tops of their heads dancing above the seats. They are as glad as he to be alone once more. Lethe leans against Lois and lies back across her. They run their hands across each other. Their faces mingle. Minutes pass. The sound of steps and they are bolt upright again. The old man beholds two sitting quietly, perfectly contrite. Can he tell that the corners of the lips are slightly upturned? Is he the butt of some joke?

That which the young share is doubly lost to us: lost because it cannot be explained or shown, and lost because we once had it and can no longer feel it. And do you know—they do not believe you were ever a child? Maybe they know you were, but they do not believe it.

I GUESS IF I'M YOUR ASSISTANT FOR THE DAY, I SHOULD tell you. I'm pregnant, said Lois.

Mandred was leaning his head against the glass, and his eyes were half-closed.

Lethe nudged her.

Louder.

I said I'm pregnant, said Lois. I have been pregnant five times already, each time with triplets. I got an award from the hospital, a plaque. I keep it with me. Do you want to see it?

Mandred was watching her now. He ran his hands through his hair.

He made a pained expression and tilted his head.

Do you know when my mother was pregnant with me she was crossing the Telfort Bridge. She was in a demonstration, a bread demonstration. My father was right beside her. But the press was too thick; people started to run and shove, and she was pushed to the edge and fell from the bridge, from one level to the next, with me in her belly. The doctors cut me out of her, out of her dead body, and I lived. I was raised by my father, who was always embarrassed that he didn't jump too, much good it would have done.

The girls looked at him in shock.

That's a joke, he said. You told a pregnancy joke, I told one too.

He closed his eyes and leaned against the window.

Lois had a book in her bag and she took it out. *The Happy Cloud*. She and Lethe paged through it. One thing about Lois that anyone can know: she volunteers with small children in the afternoons and reads to them. If you were to sail around in the air on a random afternoon, and if you flew by the place where she was, you might see her doing that, reading to children.

If she was reading *The Happy Cloud*, it would be like this: the children would be gathered around her knees, and she would tell them that a little cloud wanted to be a mountain and it made itself into the shape of a mountain, but the mountains wouldn't have anything to do with it, so it made itself into the shape of a lake, but the lakes were too far down and pretended not to notice it, and so it tried to look like the moon, but the moon was too slippery, and it couldn't look that way, not really at all, and so finally it tried to look like the sun, and the effort of that made it break up into nothing, and then it was gone. The last page includes the moral, which you are supposed to explain to the children, and which Lois always explains, with such a sweet expression on her face that anyone would believe her. If she read you *The Happy Cloud*, you might end up regretting some of your decisions. After they read, the children play games and sing songs. The songs are infectious and Lois sometimes finds herself singing them when she doesn't want to.

As Lethe looked at the book, Lois described to her the worst one.

It's about rain. It talks about how the rain falls on the tops of every building in town. It's just a list of the buildings in the town. But it's really catchy.

A BUZZER RANG IN THE COMPARTMENT.

Mandred sat up and looked at his watch.

We should be there shortly, he said. We are almost there. Just a few minutes more. A few minutes more.

He seemed a little disoriented.

Tomorrow, you know, is Ogias' Day. I'm sure it hasn't escaped you.

The girls looked at him with humor in their eyes.

Were you alive for the last one?

Ha. How old do you think I am?

Lois shrugged.

It was more than fifty years ago. I was a child then. Tomorrow there will be pavilions set up all across the city. There are rules for the day, and all the rules are different from how things are on any other day. I have the map here. Do you know what is most special about Ogias' Day?

Lois shook her head.

Lethe hit her on the shoulder.

You do.

Oh that, yeah, no one owes any money.

It is a debt forgiveness day—across the nation. No citizen owes anything. A blank slate. Do you know why they do such a thing?

Both girls stared blankly.

It brings the nation together. We all become closer.

Lethe whispered to Lois: They have to do it, or the government would fall apart.

What's that?

She said they have to do it or the government would fall apart.

Mandred laughed.

That is one way of looking at it.

He took a newssheet out of his bag and unfolded it. He leaned forward, laying it across his knees. The two girls leaned in. On the unfolded newssheet was an overview of the city center. There were indications for all the regular buildings, but also all the new pavilions, the many paper gates, the stalls.

There will be no traffic in the whole center. And the lights will stay on all through the night.

Lethe looked down at the map and she imagined herself running along the tops of the buildings, leaping from one to another. She pictured herself in the clothes she would wear, and she pictured Lois with her, sitting beneath the trees of the Fifth Rondee. They could lie in the grass and watch everyone wander by. They could even sleep there, in the out-of-doors. Maybe everyone would sleep in the street tomorrow night. Who knew what would happen? Would it be a new age?

Mandred was saying something. Lethe felt suddenly annoyed. She felt itchy all over. She wanted to be far away. What were they doing here with him? He stank. The trip was taking so long.

Did your wife really gas herself? Did she leave you a note?

Lois turned pale as a sheet.

Mandred sat back crumpling the newssheet in his hands.

What?

I said did your wife gas herself. People are saying she did.

He started to say something, then stopped. Then he started again, in the midst of some frown.

He stood up and went along the boxes of seats, off down the car.

What is wrong with you?

I just, I got tired of him suddenly.

Now we have to spend the rest of the day like this. Are you out of your mind?

Lethe ducked her head.

Are you mad at me?

Yes, I'm mad at you.

Are you still mad at me?

Yes.

Still?

Stop it.

If his wife wanted to kill herself, let her. Who cares? Now he's drinking himself to death on the toilet.

The train rattled on.

Are you still mad at me?

The two girls joined hands and stared at the wall in front of them. Across the molding were painted letters, and those letters read:

A citizen/For the life of him/Or her or he or she/That keeps a mask/On the belt or arm/Need never fear the streets.//If trouble comes/Like quad scum—/Your mask put on!/Your mask put on!//The gas shall flow/A cloud to grow/And lay them low/The lowest at our feet.

The words wound on, repeating, around the whole train car. After a few minutes the old man came back. He sat down quietly, folded the crumpled newssheet, replaced it in his valise, snapped the valise shut. The train pulled to a halt.

We're there, he said.

They got off the train and went down a long set of stairs that led to a sort of covered bridge. The inside of the covered bridge was painted with animals of every sort in once wild colors. But the paint was chipped and faded. They went along there, Mandred ahead, the girls a step behind. At the end of the bridge was a turnstile, and then a long lawn, the edges of which washed up against an old building with Corinthian columns and a wide, wise face.

That is the zoo, Mandred said.

To one side was a huge enclosure covered in netting.

What is that for?

It was for birds of prey—eagles and hawks, vultures, owls, falcons.

The words sounded strange in the air.

Did you ever see them?

I saw an owl once, when I was your age.

There were men at the door, and they told the little group that Mandred could only take one person in with him. He insisted that they should both come, but the uniformed doormen wouldn't budge.

Lecturer Alan Mandred & assistant. That's what the book says.

Mandred looked at the girls.

You will need to choose which one of you comes.

But Lethe was already wandering away to sit at the edge of the lawn.

2

L ois looked back once as they went through the gated door, and what she saw was Lethe on her back in the grass, staring upward.

Who could say if her eyes were open or closed?

Lois took the old man's arm, and they went forward through a series of vaulted arcades.

Another doorman stepped out from the shadow of a pillar.

Do you know the way?

Quite well, quite well.

The zoo building was full of mosaics of beasts. Beasts were worked in squares and inconceivable motifs into every wall and pillar; they were above every door. There was some lettering that she could not read. Mandred said it was a language no longer spoken. There are only a few buildings like this left, he confided. In an earlier time this city was also a great city, perhaps it has always been a great city. Some places are conducive to life.

They turned right at an enormous statue of a bear, and up ahead there was a large blue double door.

The animals are in there.

THERE WAS A MASSIVE KNOCKER. LOIS TOOK HOLD OF it and swung it. A loud CRACK, and the sound reverberated all along the wide stone floor. Someone from within turned a wheel that moved the massive door gradually in, an inch, two inches, three. When it had opened four feet it stopped, and they went through, first she, then the old man.

Immediately in the dim light she saw a cage, and a creature on all fours in it, covered in fur. It was a dog, she was sure. But it wasn't moving.

Past it was another cage, and this one held a cat, in a life-like pose, reaching up with a paw as if to bat at something. The cat's face was so elegant. Had she ever seen anything as elegant? But the cat was long dead.

To the left was a horse, mostly in shadows. It had once been white and now was a color of filth and time. The horse's head was impossibly large. There was no cage, and she ran her hand across the nostrils. No one stopped her.

Past the horse was the body of something like a horse, but squatter and smaller. A donkey? It seemed kinder than the horse, but its eyes were glass. It didn't know what it saw anymore.

Mandred had gone on. He called to her, over here, here.

She came along the rows, quicker, passing by cage after cage, each with its dead occupant.

When she caught up, Mandred was standing before the last cage. There was a man in uniform observing. A little light-bulb hung from a rope above the cage, and it swung ever so slightly back and forth, illuminating a small creature. She knelt down by the cage, and the creature turned its head. It turned its head!

She looked into the eyes, and looked as deeply as she could at its long ears, tried to drink in its soiled tawny fur, its little ball of a tail.

It is a rabbit, she said.

A hare, said Mandred. Probably the last hare.

Isn't there a story, an old story.

Yes, a very old story.

And then a farther door opened, and a man came, and there were greetings given. Mandred was embraced and he embraced someone. Lois stood and she too was embraced, and they were drawn along away from the dirty cage and the guard. As she passed through the next door, she felt she could feel as much as see the life that rang through the hare like a bell, a bell that was trembling, a bell struck at some point in the past, never again to sound.

AND THEN THEY WERE IN A COZY ROOM, PILED HIGH with books and papers, with figurines and sculptures, blankets, astronomical devices—whatever could be imagined to be strange, there it was. And he, the zookeeper, an older man, as thin as a broom, with wild sandy hair and a gentle manner. Could you have guessed the zookeeper would be like this? It seems he could be no other way, this keeper of the last hare.

How old is it?

His voice was raspy and thin when he answered,

We can't say for sure. Of course, we give it a kind of serum that stretches its time out. It has certainly lived longer than any other creature of its kind. It had a mate, but she died last year. I don't expect him to last much longer. My wife says I shouldn't share things like this, but . . . Every morning when I lace my shoes and come here I feel I will arrive and find its little body curled there. I have lived that moment countless times. I wish I could let you take him on your lap as I do. The feeling of an animal in your arms—it is inexpressible.

Do you do that when the zoo is closed?

No, just when I like. I bring him in here. Mostly he's in here. But lately he's been sick and just goes limp if he is touched. So I'm letting him be.

Are there other animals in other zoos? How many zoos are there?

There is a rat in the capital. There is a tortoise in Mauviers. Those are the ones I know.

Have you seen them?

Of course—and many more, but they are all gone now. We are left with the least interesting animal, man.

His voice sounded pathetic. Why are men in particular always grieving worlds that are gone? They can never come to terms with how things are.

It's not so bad. There are insects, said Lois.

Of course there are still insects, more insects than there ever were. Both original and domesticated. How else could we have trees? How else could we have fields to eat from? And there are bacteria and viruses. So I suppose man is not alone. But insects and bacteria aren't animals, are they?

I think of an amoeba as an animal.

He laughed.

Mandred spoke up.

Lois, this is Ganner. Ganner, this is Lois. Lois is my assistant for the day; she's in a section of my Historical Pathologies lecture. She and her friend accompanied me here.

Giving the introduction exhausted him. He leaned an arm on the desk. He was tired of the young women, wished in fact that he hadn't brought them. Why had he done it? It had been an idea of the morning—morning ideas were always flawed. They never take into account the accretion of weariness and grief that the late day brings. What a nasty girl the other was—or not she, but just young people in general, every one of them, so utterly selfish. Had he ever met a single person under the age of twenty who wasn't just completely selfish?

Ganner was asking him something.

Where is the friend?

They wouldn't let her in; she's outside.

It isn't really safe out there; Gall Roads is . . .

Mandred made a gesture. Something like, it doesn't matter.

Lois agreed.

Don't worry about Lethe.

As you say, as you say. Well, welcome, Lois. You have the freedom of the neighborhood, wander the building as you like . . . If you don't mind . . .

The two turned away to speak, leaving her abruptly alone.

LOIS STOOD UP AND WALKED AWAY FROM THE POOL of light that surrounded the two men. She felt at once a fondness for the enterprise, for the zoo and its husks, and its living fossil, the hare. At the same time she felt a horror, and wanted to be far away. She thought of going back to where Lethe waited, but she didn't know the way and was afraid of being lost within this massive marble tomb. Do the places we inhabit confine us by their very nature? Are we always imprisoned, eternally imprisoned, in body, in place, in community, do even our minds imprison us? What would it be like to be free, even for a second? Is that death? Do we live only in that final moment when we flee our shape?

LOIS WANDERED UP AND DOWN THE CORRIDORS, LOST
in thought. An attendant approached her.

Excuse me, have you seen a white pouch lying around?

A pouch?

Like a mailbag. A pouch. White with a drawstring.

No, I haven't.

She examined his face and he hers. They looked right into each other, almost by accident, without pretense, and then, at once, both blushed.

I'm looking for it.

He was about her age, maybe slightly older.

He smiled. Name's Strom, who're you?

Lois.

Well, Lois—what are you doing here in these halls?

I came out here from the Center today to see the zoo.

But with whom? How'd you get in?

I was just talking with Ganner in there.

The zookeeper! Very good. Poor old man. He'll be out of a job pretty soon. We all will. They're shutting the place down once the rabbit dies. Not that I've ever seen it. You know they won't even let us in there to see it? I've asked a dozen times, at least.

He trailed off.

Will you help me look for this pouch?

And with that they were gone! Off they went away from us, the pair, heads close together. He told her things and she did likewise. Their eyes ran along the ground, and into nooks and crannies, as if hunting. They did not know it, but they were late in a procession, thousands of couples who had walked in that exact line, for centuries, and though unaware, what they felt at that moment was not unlike what all these others had felt. How odd it is to think of human beings as separate—it seems so obvious, mustn't they all be one continuous crying out? A vacuum of space, and to fill it, the slightest shout of life?

If we run to catch them, we find that they know each other better. He is going to show her an atrium. It is just down that way.

WHEN YOU MEET SOMEONE, HOW DO YOU DECIDE
what you will know about them, what you will permit
yourself to know, what you would like to know, what you
would like not to know? It is only a few people in our lives
about whom we want to know everything, isn't that so?

There's nothing to do here but walk the corridors, said
the boy.

Yeah?

It's actually in my job description. We're chosen because
we fit the uniforms and because our voices and manners
are right. We have no special skills.

I would never have guessed, she said.

I mean, I can do other things—but I don't have to.

Right.

They went on and up a set of stairs that led to a balcony
overlooking a large atrium with a hill and obelisk.

Let's sit here, she said, jumping up onto the stone balustrade.

What she wanted to talk about was Ogias' Day. The
thought of it had just returned to her. While she had been
thinking thoughts of the zoo, she had been far away within

herself, but the open air and the sight of the hill and its grass brought with it a different mind. She remembered who she had been before coming to the zoo and who she would be after. Ogias' Day! What would it be like?

I am going with some friends, said the attendant. We will go to the Center. You know I, I've never been there.

Lois laughed as if this was ridiculous. Strom looked at her and looked away. He was a bit hurt.

I'm just laughing at you, she said. Why haven't you been to the Center?

What is there to do there but buy things? he said.

I guess not much. I go to school there.

How is that?

Awful. Just awful.

I was rated until twelve, and then they let me out.

Lois looked at her feet kicking in the air, and far beneath, the ground. A hose was curled by a little tree. It hadn't been put away properly. The atrium looked like no one ever went in it.

What about you? he asked.

I'm rated to twenty-six.

Twenty-six? I've never met anyone rated to twenty-six. You must be fucking smart. I better watch what I say.

Wait, but what is your base grade?

Four.

See, I'm a two. I think twelve is the max rating for base grade three and above. So you could have done the same as me on the test and it wouldn't matter.

He said he didn't know any of that. Where did she hear it?

She said they explained it in school.

He said, maybe at her school . . .

She looked at his face, which was rather finely put together. He had a small nose and large eyes, full lips. His eyes were, what color were they?

What is it you can do? she asked.

What can I do?

You said before that the job doesn't ask you to do anything but you can do things. So what can you do?

He smirked, as if at himself, and took a little cardboard block out of his pocket, unfolded it. It was a drawing pad.

He reached out, took her chin in his hand, and turned it to profile. She couldn't see what he was doing, but she heard a scratching sound of something against the paper.

What she could see was the windows on the other side of the atrium, past a dip in the hill. A woman was in a window wearing a gas mask. She had a gas mask on. Why would that be? She was very still. Ah, it was a statue. She recognized it now. The statue of Justice. A beautiful woman in a loose tunic that trembles in a stone wind with a stone sword and a stone mask. Her long hair flows down her back, and her thin neck seems almost too weak to carry all that weight. This was the ideal; each citizen must embody justice, must herself be an avatar of justice.

Done.

She turned and looked down.

He had torn out the sheet, and he passed it to her.

You *can* draw. This is so lovely.

You do think a lot of yourself, don't you?

I don't mean me, I mean the drawing is so, so professional.

I just do it, I'm always doing it. You can have the drawing. It's fine.

They sat there quietly for a while, and she put the drawing inside the book she took from her bag and put the book back into the bag, and the bag back onto the railing. She took it out again and looked at it, and then put it away just as before.

He said he heard on the last Ogias' Day a lot of people died. Everything turns upside down. Freedom surprises people—they don't know what to do with it. People who have been paying back debts for decades—and then the debt is just gone! It makes them crazy, especially if they know other people who did fuck all with their debts. And everyone's in the same boat? What is that? You could see why people would be mad.

Are you saying you think it's a bad idea?

No, no. I mean, I owe some. I've run it up pretty badly. You know, this job doesn't pay much. I'm glad for it to stop.

I don't owe anything, she said. I still live at home.

He snorted.

The smart girl who lives with mom and dad.

I heard, she said, that it isn't just debt. It's all bonds. So after tomorrow, no one is married. You'd have to get remarried. You have to reacquire your job. Everything's started over. It's a complete restart. They have to explain all this. That's why everyone has to go to the announcement points.

Can't be true. I never heard any of that. My brother says, he says Ogias' Day isn't for us anyway. It's more for people like you, people who own things. It's a holiday to keep you owning the things you own.

She laughed.

I don't own anything.

The sun had gone down, and they were practically sitting in the dark. Lois remembered Lethe waiting out in front of the zoo, and she slid her legs back over the balustrade, jumped down, and ran away down the stairs, with him close behind, calling out, Lois, Lois, what is it?

WHEN WE WANT TO GET TO SOMEONE AS BADLY AS that there are always impediments. She ran back along one hall, another. She found the place with the knocker. The door wheeled back, slower than before. She ran past all the cages, and past the last cage. The light was now turned off, although the guard was there in the dark. Through that last door. She found Mandred and he was ready to leave. They said good-bye to Ganner, and she pulled Mandred on through the doors, dragging him, but he was so slow. He couldn't see the need to run, and wouldn't. But Lethe! she said. It's been so long.

When they got to the front the doormen were gone from the gate, which was locked but could be passed through if you were going out. Out they went. Lois looked right and left, she dashed out onto the grass and turned a circle. No Lethe.

Where did she go?

Do you think she's all right?

It was very dark, and hard to see even halfway across the long lawn. The zoo was beautiful in the dimness, but Lois felt a horror in her heart, and even felt at fault. Should she have left her?

Where was Lethe?

Mandred made a show of looking, but he didn't see anyone. He said so.

Lethe!

Lethe!

Where did she go?

3

If we look for Lethe, we shall do so in a different way. We'll go back to where we left her, and when Lois goes running to join Mandred in the passage to the zoo, we will go out with Lethe onto the grass. Perhaps we should never have left her in the first place.

She went there and lay down. The grass was what grass often is: soft and endless. Her arms reached out and it happened: that wonderful thing that happens when you reach your arms out in the grass—there is enough world to meet your fingers as far as you can stretch them! As far as you stretch them, you can feel the grass and the earth, and you wriggle your feet and there is more there too!

She kicked off her shoes and lay there happily until two children came and spoke to her. Their little gas masks dangled from their necks in beautiful miniature.

What are you doing?

Just lying here, she said.

But this is our lawn, said the little girl.

Whose lawn?

Ours. We're the Fressinets.

The Fressinets?

I'm Benji, she's Lucie. And that's our dad. We come here all the time, and because we come here more than you, it's ours. Our lawn. You have to ask permission. Today Lucie is the king of the lawn. I was the king yesterday, but today she is. You have to ask permission.

She asked Lucie for permission to be on the lawn, and permission was granted. She was given a rank of some kind, which entitled her to lord it over anyone else who came. The two kids sat next to her, and all three blinked their eyes in the sunlight.

The father came up then. He was a young father. You wouldn't know he was one.

And he said, *Their mother's gone, sorry they're so attached to you, but their mother's gone.*

I'm sorry. That's hard.

The kids looked anywhere but at her.

When your mother's gone, there's not much to do but try to find a new one, even if it's just for a little while, even for an afternoon.

He spoke intently, and Lethe didn't like it. She felt uncomfortable, but she couldn't wriggle out. He was holding her in his gaze, and the children were like anchors on either side. She started to get up, but one of the kids took her hand.

Where are you going?

I was just going to go for a walk over there.

She pointed to the trees.

Okay. Lucie and I will stay here, said the man. You can take Benji to the trees. We'll see you in a bit.

The king gives you permission to go, said Lucie.

The man winked and sat down.

Have fun.

All right, Benji.

She took the child's hand; they headed for the trees, at a run.

You're much prettier than my mother was, said Benji, giggling.

Oh?

Yeah, she was not much to look at, that's what Dad says. But they got together anyway. I have a picture of her, but I'm not allowed to see it. We keep it in a box. Do you like us?

Sure I do.

They got to the trees, and she saw that there was just a shallow line of trees before a metal fence stopped any further progress. Then the forest began in earnest on the other side.

Well, that won't do us any good, she said. Here we go!

They ran to the other side of the lawn, where the old birdcage was. Inside there were many dead limbs of trees for perching on, but nothing would perch there. She said something about this to the boy, who looked at her like she had three heads.

Where are you from? Your accent is kind of funny.

From the Center.

Are you going back there?

Yeah, I'm going to go back there pretty soon. In a few minutes, I think.

Are you the same age as my mom?

I don't know. I don't know what age she is.

She isn't any age now. She's gone.

Benji clutched at her hand.

Do you like it here?

Yes, it's very nice.

We come here all the time. Every day. Yesterday we met someone like you. The day before we met two boys who hit Lucie. They were my size, but I didn't do anything.

Why?

Lucie was siding with them, and then they turned on her. So I was on my own side.

They crossed the lawn again and came to the father and daughter.

Well, I'm going, said Lethe. Nice to meet you.

That was fast, said the man.

Right, said Lethe. Good-bye Benji, good-bye Lucie.

You have to ask permission, said Lucie. From the king.

Do I have your permission to go?

Of course!

Lucie gave Lethe's leg a hug.

Lethe put her shoes on and walked away. As she went Lucie said something, something quiet, and Benji replied, *She's not like Mom. She's not like Mom at all.*

LETHE FIGURED MANDRED AND LOIS WOULD GET BACK
on their own just fine. It was crazy to sit outside the zoo
for hours. She couldn't possibly do that. Why should she?

She went along the path the way they had come, and across
the bridge painted with animals. A couple guys were standing in the middle. The passage was narrow and she had to
turn sideways to get by them. They just looked full at her
and said nothing. When she looked back they were still
watching her. One smiled, but it wasn't a smile for her to
share.

When she got to the station she noticed how broken-down
it was. Somehow on arrival it had seemed quite grand, but
now it was a hovel. The benches were even, then slumped,
then even. The way things break is so horrifying—because
things break in and of themselves. They don't even need to
be destroyed from without. The mild pressure of life, and
the world falls apart.

It was hot in the sun. She took off her sweater and wrapped
it around her waist. She sat and stared across to the other
platform. There was no one there and nothing moving. She
took out her book and leafed through the pages absently,
not reading really.

After a few minutes she heard steps. She didn't want to
turn to look because she guessed who it was. The steps were
heavy, and they came slow, one after another. They stopped

behind her. Just at that moment the train came into the station, and she felt relief. She stood and skipped forward through the doors, trying not to look frightened. But the person behind her came too.

Lethe sat in the seat immediately by the door, and a man walked past, one of the men from the bridge. He sat farther down the car. But then he stood and came and sat in the box behind her. Then he stood again and came and sat opposite her.

You don't mind, do you? he said.

She looked down at her feet, trying not to meet his gaze.

Where you going? Girl, where you going?

The train swung along on its way. The creed sounded, and she stood to say it but the man did not. He stared at her legs and chest as she chanted. She wished she'd kept her sweater on, her heart was in her throat. His hands were inches away from her, and she was terrified he would suddenly touch her, at any moment it would happen.

But the creed ended. She sat again and was practically trembling. The train pulled into the next station. She hardly knew what station it was, but she jumped up and ran off, ran onto the platform and down the steps, out into a crowded street and across it, down one block and another, dodging and bumping passersby. Her legs were just pulsing beneath her, sending her on. Her lungs were heaving. She ran and ran and ran around a corner. She leaned against a wall and almost collapsed with relief. There was no one coming. She wasn't followed. She was safe.

LETHE TOOK STOCK OF WHERE SHE WAS. ON THE STREET
right in front of her there was an open-air market selling
shabby fruit and vegetables. There was a barbershop opposite, and a pawnshop. Some children were playing a game
that was broken up each time a car came. They would
shake their fists at the cars and start again, shake their fists
at the cars and start again. The people coming and going
looked pretty beaten down. Their clothes were dingy, their
masks looked outdated. There were more people here and
there without masks, wearing the mandatory uniclothes
that changed color if they came near the gas.

She felt she stuck out. Everyone must notice her. But nobody really did, and she walked on, up one street and down
another. She was trying to find her way back to the train
station, but it was a riddle she couldn't solve, one for which
she seemed to have no tools. She ended up going farther
and farther away from the train station, wherever it was,
until she found herself at the edge of a great green expanse,
a park.

HAVE YOU EVER COME UPON A PARK IN THIS WAY—OUT on a solitary sojourn? Do you know the secret delight of possession—of feeling it is your park because you found it? Because no one you know must know of it? How fine it is to venture into such a place, where you can have every last thing without worrying what anyone else has seen or thinks.

So she was pulled—in this way—into the park. Perhaps if she had known the park's name, she wouldn't have gone. Perhaps she might have recognized it as a place to avoid at all costs. But it could as well be true that she had never heard the name, that no one had ever said it in her hearing, for why would they? Why would a person like her ever have cause to enter a place like that?

LETHE WASN'T A GIRL WHO WOULD STAND OUT AMONG other girls. But if you did happen to see her by herself, you might think her remarkable, and if you did, then even when she was back with the others she would stand out for you, apart from them all, as a special kind of girl. There was something that she didn't lose when with others, some part of herself when she was alone, and this was very attractive to those who could see such things. Whether she was pretty or not—many boys wanted to have her, and some girls too. She wasn't against this, not in either case. She was not generally afraid of much, but she was extremely cautious. If there was someone who was hers, who had been hers, hers alone, it was Lois, although she had also been with others when the two of them went out. We speak of this so you can know what she imagined was in the eyes of the boys who were speaking to her.

Lethe had entered the park. Meandering, she had lost herself in the beauty of the space. Hardly ever had she been so alone. It was a feeling that she didn't know, a feeling she loved; she found she loved it, and wanted more. There are some of us who want nothing but to be alone. Are you that way? Lethe was, and it was this moment she discovered it, in the singing green space of the hills around Gall Roads.

She had walked along the edge of a lake a great distance, where it curved and curved, and turned into a kind of bogland, forcing her back to a path that went over a raised wooden walkway. There wasn't anyone in miles it seemed, until a voice spoke up. Dead ahead of her in the middle of the walkway two boys stood. Were they younger than she? Perhaps a little. But much larger. The face of one was turned, looking past her, but the face of the one before her was clear, and he had a brand across his cheek. Neither one had a mask, and she felt the shock of recognition. Had she come suddenly to a place where there was no resistance? No path back? What was in her then?

DO YOU KNOW WHERE YOU'RE GOING? HE ASKED.

How hard it is to understand the first thing that's said to us. So full of expectation—we think one thing is said when in fact something entirely different has appeared in the air.

Lethe thought it would be a threat. She felt she would be threatened, and so she almost flinched, perhaps she flinched within. She stood and stared dumbly, forcing the boy to repeat his question.

Do you know where you're going?

I don't, she said. I was looking for the train station, and then I just kept walking even though I knew I was going the wrong way.

The boys laughed.

The train station.

It was a ridiculous idea to them. In the first place, no one ever goes to the train station. In the second place, if you were to go, you would know how to get there. It would be completely obvious. You couldn't foul it up. And here she was, this girl, in the middle of the park nowhere near the train station.

I know, she said. It's stupid.

The first boy reached out and felt the material of her shirt between his fingers. She stayed still.

I don't know about stupid, but it is funny. You see, you see, we can't even tell . . .

The other boy finished for him.

We can't even tell which train station you would be talking about. That's how lost you are.

They laughed some more, and she laughed too. It felt good. The three of them laughed about it, there on the wooden slats above the bog. Maybe she wasn't in trouble. The air was clear and clean, and the light was changing. The sun was starting to go down, and the slanting rays made the world wondrous, varied, like nothing one had seen. However many times you see this last hour of day, it is never the same.

If you tell us where you want to go, we will help you get there, said one of the boys. We'll show you the way.

At least part of the way, said the other.

At least part of the way. We have things to do too.

The trouble is, she said, I don't even know where to go. I just want to get to any train station really.

If you don't want to go anywhere in particular, then you aren't really lost, are you? said the second boy. Stupid pat. I thought you all were supposed to be so smart.

I guess not.

But you are definitely lost. So I guess that proves you do want to be somewhere, doesn't it? If you keep going the way you are, you can eventually get to a stop, stop L3. That's out the other side of the park.

It's L4.

Yeah, L4. You can get to L4. We can take you part of the way in that direction.

If you go back the way you were, then you have to get back out of the park, and through a bunch of streets. Then you can come to L5. Isn't that right?

That's right.

Maybe we can go on to L4. Would you help me? If you'll help me. I appreciate it.

The two boys drew a breath and looked at her. She looked at them.

No problem, come on. It'll get dark soon, and you should be out of the park by then. I don't know what the fuck you're doing here.

She laughed nervously.

Anyway, I'm Lethe, she said, and without thinking extended her hand.

The boys took her hand and shook it, and what happened was different from what she thought would. She hadn't thought, she had just reached out with a customary gesture, an unthinking gesture, but once she'd done it, a feeling came over her: she was surprised by her sudden revulsion, for in taking their hands she came close to touching the stumps of their lack-thumbs. She almost twitched to avoid it. Did they notice? At what age did their thumbs get cut off? What about the brand? Did they have to be branded again and again as they got older?

They said their names. She said hers again for no reason, and they went on.

LET'S PLAY A GAME AS WE GO, SAID THE FIRST BOY. IF you can pick the path without our help, then you don't owe us anything.

The other boy laughed.

And if I can't?

If you can't, then you do owe us something.

How do I know you won't just lie to me? You could always say I picked the wrong way.

Well, we could always do that.

The second boy spoke up.

Look, you're scaring her. Don't do that. It's rough enough as it is.

I'm not scared, said Lethe.

In that case, let's make it a game. Here's a crossing. Which way do you think we should go?

THEY WOUND ON THROUGH THE PARK. IT DIDN'T SEEM to her that they were making much progress in any particular way, but the boys seemed confident. They kept teasing her when she made wrong choices. Every choice she made seemed to be a wrong choice.

What are we going to do with you? You have to pick right sometime.

She brought up Ogias' Day, but they seemed not to have heard of it. She tried to explain, but it puzzled them. It didn't have to do with them, and so the idea didn't matter.

All at once as they came down a hill, there was a shout.

Three girls were sitting on the edge of a wall. They jumped down and came over. From their expressions they all knew one another. The girls were bluff and confident. The way they all wore the uniclothes made them seem like an army.

Who is this whore?

You brought a pat down here to the park? What are you two going to do to her? I didn't think you were that way.

Lethe tried to laugh and introduce herself, but she found she couldn't laugh, she was too afraid, and she couldn't introduce herself; the girls looked right through her.

Where'd you find her?

Oh, leave her alone, said the first boy. She's just lost. We're helping her out.

For what? What are you getting?

The girl turned to Lethe.

What are you giving them? Some of that?

Lethe shook her head.

They're just helping me.

You two are stupid, real stupid. You're doing it for nothing? Make her give you something.

One of the other girls came up behind Lethe and shoved her a little. Another one came from the other side and shoved her.

Leave off, said the second boy. Let her be.

One of the girls stuck her face right in Lethe's.

Make her give you the mask. She'll give you her mask. Make her give it to you.

They all laughed at Lethe's discomfort. Were they laughing in delight, or just because that's what you do? In such a situation you laugh and laugh, and wait to see what happens.

One of the boys spoke then. He spoke to Lethe.

That sounds even. We help you out, you give us your mask. Anyway, you don't need it. What would you need it for?

I don't need it, said Lethe. I just, my parents can't afford another one. I'm supposed to have it.

We don't have them. None of us has a mask. We've never had one. We just want to try it. Give us yours, and the canister. Come on.

One of the girls spat on the ground.

She's not going to give it to you. She's a pat. She hates you. She's just afraid right now, or she'd say so. Fuck her. Let's go. Let her find her own way, the little whore.

The first girl nodded.

Fine, but you two are not helping her anymore. You're coming with us. Come on, let's go.

The boys met Lethe's eyes apologetically, but they followed the girls. The five went off up the hill, and Lethe was alone again.

She breathed. She didn't even realize she'd been holding her breath. Why?

I have to go on.

There was a shout behind her, and she turned around. One of the boys had run back. He ran all the way down the hill to her and stopped short, catching his breath, hands on his knees.

If you keep going that way, he said, there is a perimeter the helmets use. There are some heated boxes they stand in and such. Should be someone there to help you.

Helmets?

He laughed. The guards. What do you pats call them?

We don't call them anything. They're just guards.

Well, to us, you know . . . I mean, I can't go near them. It'd be stupid. When I go in and out of the quad, I see them, but out here . . . no. You got to keep your distance. But that's me. You they'd love, I guess.

He looked at her and waited.

She didn't know what for.

Which way did you say?

He pointed away through the trees, some direction through the trees.

Okay. Well, thanks.

Piece of advice: you make it out, don't come back.

He ran off, and she wanted to shout after him, but there was nothing to say.

IT WAS NOW BECOMING PROPERLY DARK. SHE COULD make out the path, but up ahead it seemed darker still. A fear rose in her, and as it rose, she felt if she gave herself up to it, she would have no chance at all. She swallowed it.

Be sensible, she thought. You are safe. Just keep walking in one direction and you will get somewhere and then somewhere else and there will be a bus or train. Just keep going. Even if you have to sleep in the park, how bad is that?

Anyway, I must be able to find one of those guard stations.

She thought of her parents in the front room of their house. Her father would be getting up occasionally, going to the window and looking out, or opening the front door and going out on the steps, anticipating her, wondering where she was. Her mother would tell him to stop, but eventually they would both be worried. They would call Lois's house. Lois would say where she was last seen. Would people come to look for her? Even if they did, she was nowhere near where she had been. She would never be found.

SHE STUMBLED ON THROUGH THE DARK, UP AN INCLINE now. At the top there was a faint light. Lethe emerged onto a long open field, a rectangular basin. It was ringed by trees, were they maples? The leaves shook in the night air, and there was light away there in the distance. As she came, she heard the sound of singing, and of music. There was a fire and people around the fire. The music was unlike anything she had heard. It made her feel sad, an intense sadness, but the sadness was for herself; she felt she was at the end of her life, and this was the music of that moment.

All at once she stopped. She stood there in the grip of a terrible certainty. If she went any closer, she would be seen. She must continue, she must go closer, and then she would be seen, and when she was seen she would be taken, someone would take her, and even if she resisted, even if she gassed the first ones, even if she could gas and kill five or six of them, how many would there be? If she put on the mask, she knew she would make them angry. They would all turn against her. She felt that in putting on the mask, she would be noticed. She felt she couldn't move at all, and stood there absolutely still at the field's edge. She could never get away, no matter what she did.

But another voice came, and that voice said, put on your mask. Go along the edges, go past this fire, and keep on. Don't think of them as people. Don't speak to them. Just keep on and you will make it out of the park. Be ready to use your canister, but do it only when you have to, and keep going, keep going.

At such times she knew she was supposed to say the gas creed, to just repeat it and repeat it. That was its purpose. That was why it was hers. For a time like this.

She pictured in her mind the hate that the girls had for her. She turned it in her hands and tried it on like a garment. We are separated for a reason. I have to keep going.

But she stood still, still there, staring at the faint shapes moving like people in the distance. How many of them were there? And what did they see when they looked into this blackness? Her hand moved along her belt, and she caressed the canister that hung there.

Lethe remembered something she had forgotten. Somehow she had forgotten it, and now here it was, rising in her mind. Years before, she had gone to a fair with her mother. Where her father was she didn't know. But she and her mother had gone. Lethe had wanted to go on every ride. She had gone on every ride, and when her mother wanted to go home, Lethe wouldn't have it. She wanted to see everything one more time. She didn't want it to end. So her mother gave in, and they went back around the fair and visited every place they had gone to, and as they were coming around a tent, the way they had gone before, they came upon a body lying on the ground.

It was the body of a man who had been gassed. His face was distorted and swollen, and his eyes were burst open. It was something you had never seen, eyes burst open in this way, and it changed what you thought to see it.

His hands were choking his own throat, as if he had tried to kill himself while dying. His legs were in the midst of kicking. He had died while kicking with his feet.

If we go there to that moment, we can see it from every angle. The girl and her mother there at the tent's edge by the body. Behind them avenues and a crowd dispersing, a crowd dispersing in every various gaiety. The sound of machinery and the glow of lights. This mother and daughter stand, and before them a crippled, miserable form, motionless but indicating every possible motion. A person who was gassed, who died of the gas, is on the ground there, close enough to touch. Lethe's mother is in such shock, she does nothing to keep her from the sight, and so the little girl kneels down right over the body. Lethe kneels over the body with its burst eyes and listens for a heartbeat.

He's dead, she tells her mother. But he's still warm. Feel him, he's still warm.

Row House

*Of all the festivals there is none so
old as the Festival of the Infanta; it
might as well be a Dionysian rite—
it is as horrific as it is wondrous;
it is basic, basic at its core; and
therefore those who conduct it are
not revelers, they are human, with
the longing of all humans, to
consume, to destroy.*

**TRADITION AND CULTURE
OF ROW HOUSE**

1

THE DAY OF
THE INFANTA

Where *is* that girl? Lessen! Lessen—come out!

It was all she could do not to burst out laughing. There in the dark, she was pent and wild and radiant. She might explode, she really might, and each time her name was called, it was worse. The little girl sat knees curled up to her chest inside a cabinet, trying as best she could not to make any sound. Oh but it was too much.

Lessen! Lessen! Are you hiding?

The footsteps came closer.

Lessen!

She burst, and in laughing was discovered, and so her laughing mother dragged her from the cabinet and laughing they went. She leapt with each step.

Don't you know we are late? The most important day of your life, and you are late? Do you know how many girls would give up anything for this? Anything at all? The hope of salvation? Anything? I would hit you, I would beat you with a spoon across your little face, but you must look perfect. You must look perfectly like yourself today. It is your sitting.

The little girl giggled and tried to run away again. Her mother didn't let her, but instead laid her in her little coat, and dragged her by the arm down three shabby flights of stairs piled high with garbage, adroitly managing the narrow space, sometimes enough only for a single foot! And out past the broken-down doors of the entrance they went into the street.

ALONG THE STREET THEY WENT. HER MOTHER KNEW
everyone, and so she was spoken to from windows, out the
front of shop stalls, yelled to around corners.

Lessen hurried along after her, keeping her head down.
For the first time in her short life she didn't have any idea
what to feel. She had been chosen to be the Infanta! She
was the Infanta. What a word! She was an Infanta, the
Infanta. Which was it? There was only one. The Infanta.
People would know it now; her mother had said so, and at
that moment Lessen the little girl had gone away, replaced
by she, she alone in all of Row House. All the adults must
know and should know and did know—the Infanta! But
Lessen wasn't sure what it meant for her, and not knowing
what it meant, she didn't know exactly how to feel.

She caught a glimpse of herself in a window. She didn't look
very much different. At any rate it wasn't how she looked
to herself but what they saw. How could she know what
they saw?

Her mother was talking. She was saying: And when we get
there, remember, you must pay complete attention; there
are many things that you must remember, and if you make
any mistakes, it would be terrible. It would be truly terrible.

Lessen promised she would be careful. She was careful. She
was quiet and everyone told her she was beautiful. You are
a beautiful girl, a beautiful girl, people would say. They

would call her beautiful and stroke her hair like she was a dog. She liked it, and raised up her neck against the hand when it came, if she didn't mind the person doing it. But beautiful, well, she knew she looked like a horse. Her brother had told her many times, and she believed him. But horse-faced or not—she would be the center of the festival. Tomorrow was the Day of the Infanta! In her whole life this holiday hadn't been, and now here it was.

Her mother was rattling on. She had been saying the same things the whole evening and whole morning, and now she was saying them again. Something made Lessen listen this time. Was it the sudden force of the sunlight as they rounded a corner? The world arrives out of nowhere—and goes away as fast!

Everything they say to you is part of the ceremony. That means they do a bunch of things one after the other, and everyone knows what is to come. That's what a ceremony is—doing things in order. Since you are a part of it, they don't want you to mess it up by guessing what you should do ahead of time. So when we leave and come home no one can speak to you until tomorrow.

No one, what?

Her mother repeated it. She couldn't be spoken to until the day of the festival. That was the rule.

Lessen burst out crying. She sat down on a curb and refused to continue, sticking her legs out to either side like a soldier.

Her mother cajoled her and drew her on.

It will be okay, don't worry. It is only a few hours anyway, and then you'll go to sleep. And we can still be together; I can read to you, and sit with you in bed until you doze off. I just can't talk to you, and you can't talk to me. The same with your brother, your father, your sister. It will be fine. What I'm saying is—it is all a part of the ceremony. The festival is not just tomorrow—it's already started, but not for everyone, just for the participants. So you get more of it than anyone else does. Come on now, darling.

THEY APPROACHED A LARGE AND FILTHY BUILDING. IT seemed to be broken-down in places. There were parts of an animal, a wooden elephant, or at least its back and legs, leaned against the building.

What is that?

It's the theater.

No, that.

There was a small door next to a sewage hole. They knocked on it and it opened.

What do you want?

They went in the back door. There were many people in the dark getting dressed, getting undressed, assuming costumes, coloring their faces, shoving one another, embracing, turning their backs, kneeling, standing, exclaiming. This mother and daughter passed through them all like a whispered question, from hand to hand, mouth to ear, out into the main stage area. Immediately they were greeted with noise and light and endless space above. Lessen reeled and held to her mother's hand.

Dozens of people were hammering away on a massive float that occupied the center of the room. Others were working on costumes and props and simple machinery. Some seemed to be loitering and doing nothing. Others danced or seemed to play at fighting.

When Lessen appeared at the edge of the light a shout went up and all work stopped.

A man with a red face and a long silver coat jumped down from a stage off to one side. She had not seen that there.

He approached them.

The Infanta is here! Come, let us welcome her!

A huge roar came then in the theater, and it built and built, and Lessen could feel it inside of her and outside of her—and she did not blush or turn away but curtsied as her mother had shown her, and suddenly, impossibly, there was silence.

They were waiting for her to say something.

Tell them to continue, her mother said.

But she didn't know what to say. She stood frozen in that impossible scene, and all she could feel were her ankles and her wrists and her knees and her neck and her nose where it meets the face.

Tell them! They're all waiting.

You can continue, she said. And the tumult began again.

The man in silver bowed. He took Lessen's hands and held them up. Someone took her mother's arm and led her away. Lessen looked helplessly after her.

Don't worry, she will be near. We have much work to do, and you are to be our Infanta. Come this way. There are many people for you to meet, and all of them devoted to you.

LESSEN SAT ON A CUSHION ON A CHAIR IN A POOL OF light by the north wall of the theater. She knew it was the north wall because there was a huge N painted dead across it. *We are inside a compass,* the man had told her.

She looked straight ahead because she was not supposed to move, and looking straight ahead meant looking at a group of young men who were practicing something with sticks, broomsticks. Every one of them was covered in soot. They were, what were they . . . chimney sweeps. Her honor guard. (Tomorrow they will accompany you, and they will do whatever you tell them. Be careful what you tell them because they will do it, no matter how awful it is. You can tell them anything, and they will do it.)

She watched them and occasionally they looked over at her, and the looks in their blackened eyes could not be understood. Who did they see when they looked at her? Lessen was lost in herself—she found she had become someone she didn't know, but it was like floating. There was no effort. It maintained itself.

She stared straight ahead, and beside her there was a doll, a puppet, a papier-mâché girl of her exact dimensions. She knew that was true because they had made a hundred measurements with a tape, and also because she had looked at it and felt it was her. She liked the paper Infanta. She was fond of her. Occasionally she would sneak a look to see how things proceeded. It had been painted to have her hands and her feet. It wore the same clothes that she wore now. At that moment it was receiving her face. Her nose was appearing there, as delicate as might be, and her gray eyes, her tiny lips and ears. The brand on her cheek with its scar. Everything was there. Was that her expression? Was it really?

They brought the paper Infanta around to face her.

She looked at it and stood. The Infanta was made to stand. She sat. The Infanta was made to sit. She stood and turned in a circle. The Infanta rose and twirled.

Does she look like me? Do I look like that?

The painter bowed and mumbled something.

But do I look like that?

HER DRESS WAS OF APPLE-RED BROCADE, AND LARGER than any dress she had worn. It projected from her—she could not walk well.

Her arms were sleeved in pale white silk luminous like the bottom of a stream. Her legs the same, though you could not see them.

Her face was behind a veil of golden links that fell from a sort of corona atop her head. It was not heavy, and her hair had been braided into it, so the whole thing was fast and wouldn't budge.

One hand wore a red glove, and material was gathered at the wrist, tied with a bow. Her thumbless hand wore white, and there was material there too. What is it for?

You will know everything soon enough.

No one has ever had clothes like this, thought Lessen. At least not in Row House. She had never seen such material, never dreamed it existed. It almost made her faint to feel it.

People came and went, brushing past, darting here and there. But everyone bowed to her, dropped their heads, looked furtively from some low angle. No one would look her in the eye.

How strange, she thought. I really am a different one.

She felt a rushing in her head, like a smile at its start.

That man, she said, bring him.

She felt so powerful!

They brought the man over. What should she say?

Dance for me!

There was laughter.

The man began to dance.

Faster!

Faster!

He danced and danced—faster and faster.

It did work! She could almost not believe it.

Her expression was impassive. She watched as he danced, and she felt along the length of her this enormous costume. She had some sense that her costume was not just her clothes, but also all of the people and all the things they did. It was an intuition like destiny. Beside her stood her paper mirror, persistently reflecting.

And this man, dancing and dancing. He seemed to be getting tired.

Faster!

But it was too funny. All at once she was a child again, any child. She broke into laughter, and everyone laughed too.

What was it she was supposed to say? She tried to remember. It was something simple, something . . .

I am pleased.

He dropped to the ground and groveled at her feet. What did she think of that? The box of her face held joy and a smirk. What did any of this have to do with her?

She felt a calm wash over her. She inclined her head to the man. He jumped up bowing and went bowing back across the floor to the other chimney sweeps, and they banged their feet as he went in pride. Many of them clapped him on the back, and they took up their brooms and began again their broom dance, whatever it was, their practice.

She watched them, and felt now really that they were hers. Her own chimney sweeps. Who ever had such a thing? This was the best game of all—to be Infanta!

Someone behind her.

The director would like to speak to you. Are you ready?

She nodded but did not look in the direction of the voice. It was hard to turn with the dress on.

I WILL ARRIVE IN FRONT OF HER. SHE WILL BE SEATED. I will give her the instructions, the same way it always goes. I will say all the instructions in turn. I will not prejudice her one way or the other. I will speak as much to the doll as to she.

And again, do not become attached to her. She is like any of them—she is everyone's and no one's. What happens is outside of any control.

He came to the doorway and went through. There she was.

My Infanta. He bowed. My Infanta. I speak to you about our festival. The city awaits. Tomorrow is your day, the Day of the Infanta. The whole of Row House awaits it—your day is our life's blood. We thank you for giving it to us.

He paused and looked at his notes.

She started to speak up, then stopped.

What is it? he asked.

Why me?

It is not by chance—you and another girl, you both were born on the last Day of the Infanta.

Lessen cocked her head. Another girl?

Where is she?

The director took a deep breath.

She died last year when the helmets raided her parents' house.

Died?

Yes, she died. They gassed them all, and then they took her by the feet and knocked her head against the wall. They didn't even know who she was. It was just a raid.

Lessen started to cry but made no sound. She raised her chin. She thought that was what an Infanta did, so she did it.

The director saw all this. He stiffened with pride. He felt a sureness, a confidence in what would happen—how well all things would go.

Yes, when they did that, when they killed her, at that moment you were alone, though you did not know it. In any case, you were born to be Infanta—the day has been waiting for you to grow old enough. And you—you are doing wonderfully! Such a fine Infanta—they say there is only one, and she is always being born. You are she.

She lifted the veil back so she could see better.

That's all right, he said. You don't need to have the veil down until the rehearsal.

The what?

We will go through the schedule now.

A girl ran up and bowed to Lessen. She leaned forward and whispered something to the director. He nodded and said, Tell him he has one more chance and that's it.

The girl scurried off.

Infanta, the schedule: today we will prepare what needs to be prepared, and then we will have a rehearsal. Then you go home.

What is a . . . ?

We pretend to do what we will do tomorrow. We do that so it is easier when we do it for the second time.

She nodded.

Then tomorrow your honor guard will go and fetch you from your house and bring you here, and we will begin. The rehearsal will start in a little while. Do you have any questions?

What do I do?

I will explain it all as we go. I will be right by you, and I will explain. You only have to be yourself, because you are what you are pretending to be.

He began to turn away but turned back.

She lifted her chin as she looked at him. Did she look like an Infanta? she wondered. If someone didn't know she was?

One thing to remember, he said, the only thing, is that you have to be careful what you say because everyone will obey you.

She laughed.

He smiled. His head was inclined, but she could see his smile.

It is funny, he said. It is funny that everyone will obey, but it is also true, and it is also very serious. It is both funny and serious. We call these things comedy and tragedy.

Comedy is what's funny—and tragedy is what's bad?

Not bad—but serious. That is our festival—the Day of the Infanta.

How am I doing?

But she said it too quietly, and the director went away, leaving her to her thoughts, and her paper companion.

SHE SOON REGAINED HER SPIRITS.

I can make them do anything. What should I make them do? She thought about her sister, who was often very mean to her. The day before, when she had been chosen Infanta, her sister had hit her as hard as she could, right in front of the visitors. Her mother had screamed at her to stop, and her sister had hit her again before they put her in a side room and shut the door. Still they could hear her screaming. She wanted to be Infanta, but she was not. A great warmth overtook Lessen's being. It was especially good to be Infanta because it meant that her sister was not Infanta.

If Lessen told her chimney sweeps to pull off her sister's legs, what would happen? She imagined her sister screaming and trying to run away, and being caught, and lifted up (there were so many of them, surely they could lift a girl in the air and pull her legs off!).

She knew what her mother would say—that's fine, but then you would have no sister.

She could also have the chimney sweeps find her father's shift boss and tear off his legs. Now, that might be the thing to do. He was always keeping her father late and not letting him go home. Maybe he would be a better shift boss without legs.

She thought about what it would be like going down the street on the float, in this incredible dress, and pictured the crowds. Everyone she knew would be there. Everyone would see her, and they would learn that she was someone they never thought they would meet. Who was she?

She thought some more about her sister's legs being pulled off. But I wouldn't do it, she thought, I might let her think I would, though. She should know that I could do it, but didn't. She should at least know that.

THE MAGISTRATE WAS PUTTING ON HIS BEARD BY THE footlights. It was an enormous beard, twice as long as he was tall, and it was quite difficult to put on. A young woman was helping him, and occasionally he would pull her to him and run his hands along her waist and up her sides. She would squirm away, and it would all continue.

Up came the director.

Did you see her yet?

Yes—she's there on the far side. What's she like?

Spot on so far.

The magistrate pulled the young woman into his lap again. This time she let him.

He is terrible, she told the director. I'm just trying to get his beard on, and he won't let me.

You need your beard for the rehearsal. Let her put it on you. Then get on the float where you can watch the Infanta and see everything she does and says. Don't you know your work?

The magistrate laughed.

No one wants the task I do, no one's strong enough to live with it—and so I have conditions.

Yes, yes. Well, get your beard on and then do what you like.

The director continued on. Behind him, he heard the young woman:

And would you really condemn her? Condemn a child? Would you really do it? If you felt it was right?

A MAN IN A LONG, DARK COAT WAS WAITING FOR THE
director and stopped him as he came.

We just got word. The guards are going to interfere.

He pulled out a map. They looked at the route as it was
drawn.

So we were going to go this way and this way. That's the
way we've always gone. But the helmets, they'll put up barricades here and here. So I think we go this way at the start,
and we start earlier.

He pointed with his forefinger.

Then we can avoid them entirely. By the time they move
the barricades, it'll be too late. And once the crowds are
out, they can't do anything anyway.

The two men nodded.

It's just—public opinion. The pats don't like it; if they do
us in, it's one thing, but if we do us in, it's another. They'd
love to gas us all and be done. For them anything's a provo-
cation. Especially what happened before.

The director smiled.

I was director five years ago, as you know. I think this Infanta won't be like the last. Probably won't go that way. But

hard to say. The magistrate's been flogging himself since. It's hard to live with. But we always know—it can happen. It is as much a part of it as anything.

The man with the long coat took a brooch out of the collar of his shirt. The brooch was on a chain. He opened it. Inside there was a little knucklebone.

I was in the crowd when we dragged her down, he said. However it goes—it goes right. If the guards don't stop us first.

LESSEN'S MOTHER SAT IN THE BALCONY AND WATCHED it all. Her face was covered in tears. She couldn't stop crying, and she was frightened almost to death. She was shivering and crying. A man had covered her with a blanket. That's what it was like to see this woman—she looked such a sight that someone would just cover her up for no reason.

Away there she could watch the float, and she saw they were bringing Lessen onto it. She looked radiant in her dress, like a festive lantern. Where was the little girl her mother knew?

Her heart sank. It was an immovable dread that stood over her and stiffened all her thought. If only Lessen were more like her brother, then things would be fine. But she was wild, too wild. Oh, how could it have happened? They should have hid her at birth.

Her mother started to cry again and laid her face in her hands. It was useless, useless. She tried to peer down again, but everything was blurred. She could hardly see anything. She rubbed her eyes. She tried to breathe.

A man sat in the row beside her. Could she get away from him and down to her daughter? She had tried before. Then he caught up at the stairs and she thought he would hit her, but he didn't. He just dragged her back by the neck of her coat.

She looked over and the man was looking at her. Was it pity in his eyes? Not exactly. Nothing is pity, is it, not exactly?

OUTSIDE THE BACK ENTRANCE ONE OF THE COOKS WAS peeling something. He had a bucket and a bunch of the thing. Next to him was another bucket. To do his job he'd get something in his hand and peel it and then throw it in the bucket it hadn't come out of. He did this all with just one thumb, which is a kind of parlor trick, unless you're used to seeing it, and then of course it's not.

Next to him was another cook. But this cook wasn't doing anything.

One of them was saying something using everything he had that was small and awful. It had to do with his unhappiness at being a cook. The other one ate it up and even giggled. He loved being a cook, loved peeling, loved sitting outside. What a day!

But it's awful, it really is, it's awful to take a child out of her life and make her be the headpiece of this disgusting spectacle. Decade after decade it continues. You'd think we were in the Middle Ages. You'd think no one could read and everyone did what the king says, et cetera et cetera.

I don't know, I love all the holidays. I like this one especially. It isn't always bad. Sometimes everything is—well, when they say she is serene, then there is no trouble, none at all. It was like that once when I was a boy.

I don't remember that. To me it's just mayhem. Listen to yourself, *you love holidays*. What garbage. You're peeling those wrong. Here, let me show you.

The second cook did some peeling. Maybe he was better at it than the other guy.

Did you see her, though, did you see her when they brought her in? They wrapped her up in everything they could find in the wardrobe that fits a child. Then they shove her out into the street like a windup toy. It's disgusting. And the parade itself, it's just beyond reason—all the old set pieces and the actors rambling on.

The first cook shook his head very distinctly.

Whatever you think about the parade, he said, the crowd is something to see—once it goes off—once no one knows what is to happen. I bet whatever you say, you'll be there watching. Where else would you go? What else would you do?

BACK INSIDE, EVERYONE WAS SAYING, IT'S TIME, IT'S time.

On the float, there was a man with an enormous beard. Lessen laughed and skipped to him, at least as well as she could skip in the dress. She tugged at the beard and smiled up at the man, who bowed to her and covered his eyes.

You are too bright a sight for me, he said.

She went on along the float, and there was a throne of thistles and vines.

Do I sit here?

Yes.

With help she climbed up onto it.

Tell that one to come up here.

She pointed out one of the sweeps.

This one? No. This one? No. This one?

He came up onto the float.

I want him to stand here in case I need him.

All right.

A girl came and tied a ribbon around his arm.

Then there was quiet; the director was there: he stood beside the throne. The magistrate away behind. There were many young women in dresses inferior in color and make, like echoes to the Infanta.

The float had a sort of stairway at its front that led up to a flat place before the throne.

This is the Court of the Infanta, whispered the director. We go through the streets, and anyone may present a case. When they do, you listen. Then you decide how it is to be. Your sleeves are the verdict.

She looked at him in puzzlement.

Your sleeves say what you mean. One is for guilt, for those who have done bad things, this is the red sleeve, and one is for innocence, for those who are good, who you want to go free, this is the white sleeve. To make a decision, you unfurl one and raise it for the crowd, like this.

He showed her.

And if the decision is not like that—if it is just choosing between two things or people, then you use this.

He took a yellow scepter like a snake out from under the throne.

With this you point to the one you choose.

She nodded and held it in her hand. But she was confused. She felt a sudden fear. Director!

She whispered, Director, come here!

He put his head close to hers. He smelled like, she didn't know what. Something thick and . . . she didn't know.

Yes, Infanta.

How do I choose?

You'll see. You just decide. It doesn't matter. You just say what you feel.

I want to see my mother.

She has gone home. She's not here anymore. You'll see her tomorrow, after the festival.

The Infanta began to cry.

She said she would read to me. I want to go home.

Some things have changed, said the director. We need to keep you here tonight. Don't worry, there are many people to read to you.

One of the Infanta's maids came up and caressed the child's face. She was very lovely. She touched the tears with her fingertips.

Lessen stared.

This is Ari, said the director.

Call me Ari or Arianna—whatever you want. I will stay with you through the whole thing. I won't leave your side.

Lessen climbed out of the throne, and Ari held her for a while. The chimney sweep was there too, and he took her little hand in his.

Don't worry, my love, he said. We will be here with you.

IT'S TIME, THE DIRECTOR WAS SAYING. PLACES, PLACES.
We'll move the float just as it would go.

To Lessen he said, There will be real cases, real verdicts, and also ceremonial ones—prearranged ones. It is part of the festival. These cases come before every Infanta, and the crowd knows them—knows how they go. We'll go through the ceremonial ones now, one by one, so you learn what to do.

I don't understand.

Don't worry.

The float began to move. Lessen adjusted herself on the throne, which shook a bit. Her dress felt suddenly uncomfortable. She wanted to tear off her corona and veil. She wanted to run out of the theater and far away.

But who was this coming up the steps? A man painted all in gold, in gold all over—wearing no clothes but gold paint. And then a man in silver.

From the left came someone Lessen hadn't seen. He had a long pole, and he stopped the two men right before the throne.

Who are you? he said.

I am the sun, said one. I give all light. You know me.

And I am the moon, said the other. I am your companion through all of life. I am never far away, and like you, I change. You know me.

The man with the pole spoke up.

What is your grievance?

LESSEN WATCHED THE MEN AS THEY RAISED THEIR ARMS and spoke, as much to the crowd as to her. They said many things she didn't understand, but some of it she did. The sun was unhappy because the moon was sometimes coming out during the day, and he wanted the day for himself. Was that it? The moon was not unhappy, he wanted to keep on as he had been—wasn't it how it always had been? He kept saying that.

And then everyone was quiet, and then they looked at her. Was it her turn to speak?

She had the snake rod in her hand. It was very light. She looked at the sun and she looked at the moon and she thought that she didn't like the man who was the sun. His voice was loud, and he seemed very demanding. He reminded her of her uncle, who had spanked her just the week before for breaking a plate. And she hadn't even broken it. At least she hadn't put it there at the edge of the table, which was the same as breaking it. She hated him. It made her angry to think about it. Now she was sure. The moon, he was all right. But she didn't like this sun at all.

She pointed to the moon, and the crowd erupted in applause. The chimney sweeps ran up the stairs and set hands on the man in gold paint. He tried to get away, but they caught him. They carried him off shrieking to some place she couldn't see. The moon bowed like a dancer, and she let him kiss her hand. And then the float was moving on.

IT WENT TWICE AROUND THE ROOM, AND THE CROWD did their best to get in its way, as they were supposed to. Once, someone got caught under one of the wheels and had to be pulled out. At some point the director yelled and everyone halted.

Up the steps to the Infanta's Court came the biggest woman Lessen had ever seen, and she was dragging a very small man by the hair, thump, thump, thump, up the steps. He kicked his feet, but it didn't matter, he came. He had no choice.

She threw him down like a sack of flour, and he scrambled about ineffectually and bowed and scraped before Lessen. A laugh came from the director.

The woman curtsied, which looked strange from a woman so large.

What is your grievance?

It's this old shit, said the woman, kicking the man, who was on his hands and knees. He howled and looked pleadingly about.

What has he done?

He won't keep it in his pants. He runs about town knocking up this girl and that girl, and then they come to the house looking for handouts. To be plain—he sleeps around, with anyone who'll have him, and I want the old goat put out to pasture.

The crowd burst into laughter. Some threw things at the man, who was palpably struck and rolled over onto his back.

Do you have anything to say?

The man with the pole prodded the accused, who got to his feet, shook himself off, dusted himself down, adjusted his coat, took a hat out of his pocket, unfolded it, and placed it on his head.

The woman had been speaking mostly to the crowd, but the man spoke directly to Lessen.

Your Grace, I have to tell you, the burden of living with this woman for thirty years would drive anyone away. A man like me, a good man; he shouldn't have to be looking over his shoulder every minute. Every minute of every day of thirty years. That's a lot of days, a lot of minutes. She has no kindness in her, none at all. I have my failings, and I, I happen to be a person who needs some kindness now and then. I apologize for that. I apologize for being a gentle man, a gentleman who needs some kindness. And he finds it in places. He finds it in different people. But is that a crime? I'm sorry for what has happened. Truly I am. Infanta, she beats me night and day with a stick.

Not enough! said the woman. Clearly it hasn't been enough.

The woman took a step closer, and the man with the pole pushed her back.

Infanta, what shall we do with him? Help me.

Lessen didn't know what was wrong with sleeping, and she didn't know what it meant to put someone to pasture. She did think the woman was frightening, though. And the old man was so smelly. He reached out to touch Lessen's foot, and the man with the pole slapped him away.

He is guilty, said Lessen, and dropped her red sleeve.

The crowd roared, and the large woman leapt with glee.

The old man darted off past the throne and tried to dodge away through the crowd, but from the sound of it, he didn't get far. Some overzealous people began to beat him.

This is the rehearsal, shouted the director. Go easy.

THE FLOAT WENT AROUND AND AROUND, AND THIS
time it stopped so suddenly, it lurched forward, nearly toss-
ing Lessen from the throne. Someone was under the float.
There was screaming, and then a figure was pulled out
from below by the crowd. He was pulled up onto the float
and laid there before Lessen, but she could not see his face,
for his head was entirely covered by a giant gas mask and
to his hands were tied a sort of bellows. He was a mannequin, like the one they'd made of her!

A woman dressed in rags ran up the steps and dragged the
man in the mask down to his knees. She stood beside him,
pushing his head down with her hand.

Because he cannot speak, she said, I will speak for him. I am
the poor of Row House. He is the spirit that hounds us. Out
in the nation, he walks in a thousand thousand bodies, and
every one of his thousand thousand arms and all the perfect
hands, they clutch at the gas and they point the gas at us.

She took a breath; she was almost crying.

Beneath this hideous mask,

And here she kicked the man, who took it and didn't move.

I said, beneath this hideous mask, he never cries about
what he's done. The holes dug a hundred feet deep are full
of bodies. My body is thrown into a hole, again and again,
and beneath his mask he doesn't cry, and his perfect hands

point at me. He poisons me. He watches me thrash. This is a story of a hundred years, of two hundred years. These are our lives. Even now he wants to kill me, to use me. Look at him.

The crowd was full of anger. People were shouting things. Lessen couldn't hear what. Her eyes were full of the crouching man.

Infanta, I beg you. Tell me what to do. What shall we do with him? We who have him finally before us, what do we do?

A moment passed, and another.

Lessen was frozen.

The director nudged her.

The Infanta started to stand and faltered. She slipped forward. Someone steadied her, and she drew herself up quite elegantly and unfurled the red sleeve.

The woman turned to the crowd and shouted, She has no words, but justice, justice from the Infanta!

They threw the body down into the crowd, and this time the director jumped forward immediately.

Take care, take care, he cried. We'll need that for tomorrow. I'll have your heads if you wreck it now.

THERE WERE SEVERAL MORE CASES BROUGHT, AND IT was all very exciting, but also tiring, and when the director called a halt to it, Lessen was relieved. She practically had to be carried. In fact she did have to be carried, but there were many people to do it, and all of them wanted to.

Someone brought her food to eat, and someone else took her to a toilet. They didn't notice that she had peed a little in her dress, which was good because Lessen didn't think that mattered so much. Most clothes could take a little pee and nothing changed. But everyone always made such a big deal out of it. Why? It was unfortunate to pee in such a nice dress, but it was so big and thick. It didn't matter, did it? Someone gave her a cake from a little bag, and when she ate it, they gave her another. Someone helped her off with her dress and into her old clothing. Someone read her a book and sang songs with her. She wanted to speak to her mother on the telephone, but they wouldn't let her. When she cried someone held her.

Everyone kept saying what a good job she was doing and how proud they all were. Even the old man who had been beaten came to say she had done a good job. Perhaps he hadn't been beaten after all. He and the large woman waved as they went off across the theater, and Lessen felt buoyant. Who was she—and how suddenly she had become this person, she didn't know who or how!

Come this way, said a man. We have a place for you to sleep.

ONE THING IS IMPORTANT, SAID THE DIRECTOR, KNEEL-ing by the pallet. You may have dreams tonight. And if you remember them, it will be a great help to us. The dreams of the Infanta are useful. In the procession we will tell them like stories, and spread them through Row House like gossip or song. Do you remember your dreams?

Lessen said that she always did. She remembered every one. Should she tell him some?

No—tomorrow will be enough. And something else. Here in the theater it hasn't been so bad, has it, with all the performers?

And of course, it hadn't been so bad. Lessen said so.

Well, tomorrow we will be out in the streets and the crowds that come to enjoy the festival, they are really something, they are something unpredictable. Have you ever seen the ocean? Have your parents shown you pictures?

Lessen shook her head.

Well, it is water I'm talking about, as far as the eye can see. The crowd is like that, too. It is more than you can take in, and so I am saying to you, just don't worry about it. You don't have to know what's going on. I never do.

The director went away and Lessen felt afraid. Was she alone? There were so many people near. How could she be alone?

Where was her family? The theater was enormous and dark. She looked out into the darkness, and there was nothing there. Now and then a light flickered, a match being lit or a lighter, and it was as if the space, all of it sprung into being and then disappeared again. There were people lying down all over, but none were close enough, none touched her, none spoke to her. She felt alone, and the feeling gathered and twisted like a rope. Why couldn't she go home?

My darling! Here you are!

She knew that voice. She sat up.

It was Arianna, who had come back. The young woman had a flashlight, and she knelt by Lessen's pallet.

Hold this for me, would you?

Lessen held the flashlight.

Ari put some blankets on the ground next to Lessen's pallet. The man was there too, Lessen's chimney sweep.

Ari started unbuttoning her dress. The man began to lie down.

Not in front of the child, said Ari. You sleep on the other side.

Right, he said, and went around.

Tell her a story. I forgot something; be right back.

Ari disappeared into the air.

You know, I'm usually a mechanic. Do you—the man looked to see if Lessen was listening; she was—do you know what that is?

You fix things.

That's right, things that move. So one day I am repairing this bus, it's a big job, and we have the bus up on a lift, it brings it up in the air so you can work underneath it, and we discover that someone has taped a whole bunch of money to the bottom of the bus. There's just a lot of money there, a whole bunch. Me and this other guy, Hackett, we find it. So Hackett took half and I took the other half, and we didn't tell anyone. That's a secret.

Lessen's eyes widened.

What did you buy?

I didn't buy anything yet. Hackett said you should wait a long time before using money like that, and I don't need it right now. I got home and the first thing I thought was, where should I put it? Which is funny because that's the same problem the other guy had.

Lessen didn't understand.

I mean, whoever's money it was. They hid it in the bus, to hide it. I guess they didn't figure anyone would lift a bus off the ground.

And then Ari appeared with a glass of milk and some more of the little cakes.

Here you go!

Don't leave again, said Lessen.

I promise I won't.

Ari took her dress off in a way that was perhaps not so el-egant and revealed that she was the sort of girl who strives for grace but does not naturally have it. Her body was very wonderful, however. She took the flashlight back and stretched out next to the pallet. She was much prettier than Lessen's mother, who would never wear a slip like that where people could see. Lessen felt small.

Ari reached up and touched her face.

If you need me, just tug. I'm right here. And Rez is on the other side. Either one of us will help you—or even if you don't need help—if you just want to talk or have company. We're here.

The little girl tried to think of something to say. She didn't want the conversation to end.

Do you think they will let me keep my dress?

I don't know. They must—it was sewn just for you. Who else could fit in it?

Lessen climbed down from the pallet and curled up in the blanket with Ari.

She switched off the flashlight, and the theater creaked like a ship. All around there were voices murmuring, and here and there things glowing, who knows what or how. Lessen buried her cheek into Ari's neck, hiding her face like a criminal.

My little dear, said Ari, stroking her hair. My sad little darling.

IN A ROOM ABOVE, THE MAN WHO WAS TO PLAY THE magistrate, the man who had played the magistrate three times before, the man who felt he would never cease to play the magistrate, although he was not a magistrate, hated magistrates, he sat with his beard wrapped around him like a cloak. He had two empty bottles, one to the left and one to the right. He sat in a chair, and opposite him in another chair sat the paper Infanta. He was giving her a long lecture.

I know you have your charms, and I know that you are for the most part a very comprehensive version of a child, but there are secrets I must share with you, and one is: you may not be enough. You are not always enough. So you must try to do your job as well as you can. You must be as much a real girl as you can be, and when the crowd gets their hands on you and tears you to bits, you must scream and scream, and wriggle and tremble. You must go stiff and weep like a board. You must bleed if you can. Because there is a rage in the crowd, and if you cannot bear it all, if you cannot . . .

A woman in a gray skirt came into the room then. She peered around and then switched on the overhead light.

Giving her the speech, eh?

She walked around the seat from which the Infanta stared flawlessly forward. Her face was clean and full of hope. Her eyes glistened and did not blink.

You have no fear. But it will be a long day, the woman said, patting the doll on its childlike shoulder.

LESSEN WOKE IN THE NIGHT AND SAT UP. WHERE WAS she? It was somewhere she had never been. She drew up her lungs and shoulders to scream, but then a slight familiarity touched her. Who was this warm person? She remembered everything, and yet the strangeness of the theater, with its endless, never-to-be-seen ceiling and its strange miasmas, left her trembling. She felt pressed against the ground, and she pulled at the woman on the ground, who woke, and sat up, saw what was going on for what it was, and curled herself around the little girl.

Lessen began to cry, and as she cried, she became sadder and wilder, and more helpless and almost angry, and then completely weak and empty and then sad again. They lay there, and the little girl whispered in the woman's ear.

What will it be like tomorrow?

Ari lay flat on the ground wrapped in the thin blanket, and Lessen was now above her looking down, their faces as close as can be.

I remember the last festival. It was burning hot. I woke that morning and I was covered in sweat. I must have been twelve, eleven or twelve. Everyone had already left the apartment, and when I went out into the apartment block it was empty too. But when I got to the street, a wave of noise rolled over me, and there it was: the mob, so many people you can't begin to know who is who or how or why. And what's more, you join them. You run into the crowd, and it is all elbows and arms and legs. You aren't crushed, it isn't that way at all. In fact you don't even have to hold yourself up anymore. The crowd carries you, and one moment you are in one street, the next moment in another. You don't control anything. You just find yourself places, and you shout when people shout, scream when people scream. When there are things to throw, you throw them. If people, you weep. You are less alone than you have ever been, and in the midst of all that, something is cutting through the crowd, coming up the street, and it is a wooden ship fifteen feet high, and on it there is something happening. What is it that is happening up there? What is it?

Ari caressed Lessen's face, and Lessen wormed in closer.

But why me?

It's because, because they don't know what you'll do. No one knows what you might do. That's what being a queen is.

2

THE DIVERS' GAME

I t was like this, they would say something like, *Tell us where he is*, and then the boy would spit or say nothing, or look away, and then they would hit him or throw him against a wall or stamp their feet. Then there would be more of the *tell-us-where-he-is-ing* and more of the hitting, more of the stamping. They weren't hitting him very hard, were they? He was just a boy, an older boy certainly, but a boy all the same. And the two of them were men, and rather large men at that. Maybe they weren't actually hitting him. Maybe they were just threatening him. They kept saying they'd hit him. That was it. From outside the door it sounded bad. Yeah, sooner or later it was going to start, just you bet.

In the hall, one of the two men was talking to someone. He said,

We don't know yet. He won't say. Don't worry. There's nothing to worry about yet. They're just kids. He'll turn up.

This man had yellow hair like old garbage and a very loud voice. He was fatter than you would want him to be, and he came up very close to the people he was speaking to because he knew they didn't like it. We can say that he smelled just fine, though. His feet were small and he moved rather quickly. All in all a hard man to deal with.

He went back into the room.

The boy was sniveling and sitting on the edge of a table. When the man came back in he stopped sniveling, like, some kind of pride or something. He thought better of it, though, or lost control, because a few more snivels came.

Why does it have to be so hard? You were taking care of Ollie. That was your job. For the day you were to take care of Ollie. So where is he? Where is the boy you were supposed to take care of?

At the other end of the room there was another table, and the second man was sitting at it writing something down. He stood up.

Do you think anyone cares about you? The reason you were allowed in this house in the first place is because you were Ollie's playmate. He looked up to you. How's that?

The first man pulled the boy's feet and dumped him onto the ground. The boy's back and head rapped against the floor, and he cried out.

I'm sorry I did that, said the man.

He helped the boy up.

I'm really sorry.

He shoved the boy and the boy fell down again. The man yanked him back up to his feet.

I'm sorry I did that. We just, we want you to tell us where Ollie is. You won't tell. Come on. Why won't you.

I don't know. I don't know where he is! We were supposed to meet by the statue at Garstal and Matby. Maybe he's there.

You said that already, but we know you weren't there. Don't lie. You think we don't know what we know—but you don't know how we know what we know or who tells us things—it'd break your shitty little brain. So just come clean. Tell us the truth.

It's not a lie. I said we were supposed to meet. I didn't say I went. We were. We were. Why don't you go check the statue? See if he's there. I'm telling you. It's all the truth. I told you. Why don't you believe me? Yesterday morning I came here, I picked up Ollie. He said he wanted to go to the arcades. He loves it there. We go to the stalls his father owns. He sinks them, seven at a time, and we can make it all back and more. Every time we've gone down there, and

it's no problem. Last week, the week before, the week before that. You know—you've seen me bring him back. You
know. So we went down there, and we were there for some
hours, and when I looked for him he was gone. Just like
that. I went through every stall, and he wasn't there. I didn't
ask for help because maybe he didn't want to be found. I
don't know. When we first got there I told him meet me
by Garstal and Matby if we get separated, but then when
we did get separated he didn't come. Or at least Satler said
he didn't show up. I mean, you're right that I wasn't there.
I wasn't. I left Satler to meet him. What's wrong with that?
Satler's his friend too.

What's wrong with that?

The man shook his head.

That was three o'clock, the boy sniffed. Three o'clock! He
could be anywhere by now. That's not my fault. You got to
let me go. I didn't do anything. Do what you want to my
dad, he's a louse, but let me go.

The men looked at each other. The yellow-haired one waited
for the other to decide.

The second man wrote something in his notebook. He
nodded.

What do you think?

A third man was sitting on the floor by the window. His shoes and shirt had been pulled off and were tied around his neck, who knows why.

Briggs, what do you think? He's your son, is he lying?

I don't know. He lies all the time. I'm really sorry. You got to tell Mr. Spencer how sorry I am. I just didn't know the boys were doing this. I didn't know they were going off alone. Tell Mr. Spencer that, I mean, he's got to know that. Eben, tell them where Ollie is, please tell them. Don't you understand what's happening?

Briggs, if this is some blackmailing scheme, I'm telling you, we will dump your body in a bush somewhere. No one cares.

Briggs let out a wail. He insisted it was no blackmailing scheme. If it had been, wouldn't they have worked it out better? And anyway, Eben was just a wild kid. Ollie was too. With the two of them, who knew what they'd been up to. Ollie was probably fine. He would be back any minute, walking in the door. Briggs tried to make them see it—Ollie would just walk back in the door and everything would be fine. Like it was any other day but today.

Chester interrupted him. He tapped his notebook against his wrist impatiently.

When does your wife come back to the house?

My wife? Ughh. Ah, usually, she, she would be there about, ah, no, but today—it's the parade, so, she might not be back for hours, maybe not till the nighttime.

Do you know where she is? Maybe she can get something out of this clown.

He aimed a kick at the boy, who was now on the floor, but the boy cringed and the foot stopped short.

All right then. There's nothing for it. Garstal and Matby. Let's go.

THE BOY PICTURED THE MAN WITH THE YELLOW HAIR standing too close to a window, and he imagined himself shoving the man out. How that would be! He'd just laugh and laugh and maybe even call something after him. What would be the best thing to say?

THEY GOT OUT TO THE STREET, AND THERE WERE HEADS as far as the eye could see. Not even bodies, just heads. Some wore hats, some wore glasses. Some were high up, others lower. The heads jostled and trembled, and sometimes waves passed through when something exciting or terrible happened nearby. It was a crowd, and it took up all of that street and all of the next street and all of the street after that. If that were the world, it would have stopped there, but it didn't, it went on, street after street. The parade was coming. The parade was somewhere nearby. They were in the parade. The parade had happened. It was about to happen. Had anyone seen it? There was a rumor someone had seen the procession a few blocks north, and that set off a ripple that trampled two people so badly, they had to be pulled to the edge and laid on a stoop. But some did go a few blocks north, and who knows, maybe it came to nothing. Carson and Chester elbowed their way through and dragged Eben after them. It was a sign of something that they could make any progress at all.

First they went along DeKhan Street as if they were headed to the bus depot, but at Wessel they took a right. Carson's grip on Eben's wrist was like iron. There was no chance he could wriggle out, so he skittered after the two men as they marched resolutely forward, elbowing and shoving their way.

Of all the fucking days it had to be, said Carson.

What, you don't like a parade?

They came around the corner of Wessel and Averbeig, threading their way through food vendors and stalls selling fake gas masks and flags with anything on them. That's when Eben saw it.

The parade! Look.

IT WAS COMING DOWN AVERBEIG, THE GROUCHERS were running there with their brooms, hitting whoever came close and clearing the path. The float was a greenish white color and covered in scales of some cheap material that glimmered like eyes. Atop it were dozens of people in costumes, and there at the front, a throne, and on the throne, the Infanta! She was all in red, and she stood out from the parade like a lacerated cheek. She was pointing a scepter, and the grouchers were doing whatever she said. It just got worse wherever she pointed. Some people were running in a stampede away from the float, and Eben wondered why. Was it better to be close or farther away? But he saw the grouchers were dragging people onto the float and stripping off their clothes. The Infanta was jumping around. No one could stop her. She pointed out an old woman, and they pulled her up onto the float and the Infanta made her crouch on all fours and howl. People hung from windows and shouted with delight. Others began to break down the doors along the street and rush into the houses. A painful wrench on his arm: Eben was pulled around a corner, and that was the last he saw of it.

We'll go down that alley. There are too many people—this is exhausting. I mean the old man says do it so we'll do it, but it is no fun.

You having fun? Carson asked Eben.

No.

Because if you were, I'd say I'll break your fucking arm.
We better find Ollie soon, or you'll regret it. Thing is we
know you had it in for him.

Chester nodded.

He told his father. He said you didn't like him. Said you
and your other friend . . .

Satler, said Carson, chiming in.

Yeah, Satler. You and that little prick were always giving
him a hard time. Spencer said should we do something
about it, but Ollie said no. He'd work it out, and that's
right. That's the right way to handle it. But then what happens? Where's Ollie? No one knows.

Maybe this shit knows, said Carson. I think he and his
fuckup dad want a payout. That's what I think.

Do you want a payout? Do you?

They came to an alley that ran behind a hospital. Through
a window they saw the beleaguered face of a nurse.

Bad day to be a doctor, said Chester.

Funny for you to say it. The man practically keeps them in
business. Here now, here we are.

They crossed a road that had been blocked off but was now mostly empty, and passed over a freight crossing to something like a meat market. Beyond it was the broad entrance to an abattoir—the famous slaughter yard, now in disuse. It was full of garbage, just a dump.

Past that, they came to a square. There was a statue of a man with an enormous top hat.

Well, here we are.

ONE WALL OF THE SQUARE WAS COVERED IN MURALS.
The murals showed heroic guards in gas masks standing in
great swirling clouds of yellow and green. The faces of people with branded cheeks were in various states of discomfort and death at the guards' feet and wherever the smoke
curled to show what lay beneath. Of course, all three had
passed it so many times, they could no longer see it.

That's the statue, said Eben. Maybe . . .

But the entire square was empty. There was no one there.
No one at all.

The two men sat heavily on the steps.

We're going to have a talk, said Carson, and something
good better come out of it.

CHILDREN DON'T LIE. NO CHILD HAS EVER TOLD A LIE.
Because the world they live in is not the same one we inhabit. So if all of the things they know are different from all the things we know, then how could they lie? In essence we are always talking about one thing when they are talking about another. What they can do is try to make life as nice as possible, and they do this by trying to identify the things they can say that might convince anyone with any wherewithal to make things better. Children are just water flowing downstream. There is no meaning to be taken from their words.

What's more—adults are the same way! We are all just desperate to have more of what's nice, and we'll say anything to get it. We'll do anything, be anything, say anything, just in order to reach the world that we believe in. Even selfless people do this—the world that they want to reach is just one in which they're punished.

So if that's how things always are, then what could it possibly mean to say that one thing is a lie and another thing is true?

Something like this was running through Chester's head as he sat there on the steps. He took out his notebook and wrote on it the words

Four o'clock. Spencer.

He showed this to Eben.

Can you read? Can you read, Eben?

Eben looked at it.

That's what happens at four P.M. We take you to Spencer, and god knows what he will do. If you don't like us, if you know us and don't like us, well, let me tell you, you don't know Spencer and you won't like him, not what he'll do. He assured me in the hall, didn't he, didn't he just, he said, I know the boy and his father are up to something. Find it out. You know your father owes Spencer a lot of money. Who owns your father's store?

My father.

Wrong. Spencer owns it. Who owns the merchandise in that store?

My father.

Nope. Spencer owns it. And who has to deal with the short-fall when your idiot father loses money every month for the last two years? So now you see—it really does look like it. And that's what Spencer knows. That's what he knows about you.

Which brings us around to the question again, said Chester. Where are you keeping Ollie? Does your mother have him? We tossed your house. He isn't there.

Tossed the house? laughed Carson. We tossed the whole damn street.

Eben looked very small standing beneath the two men who in turn looked tiny beneath the statue with its huge hat, and the statue was made small by the blocks around it and the quad, and the quad was made small by the green fields around it, the high fences, the city beyond, and the city was small in the vastness of debris and devastation that is the world, and of course, the world was the smallest of all, the very smallest, for if you get even a little ways away, you wouldn't know it was yours. You wouldn't have the first idea how to get back to it.

ALL RIGHT, ALL RIGHT. THE BOY WAS TALKING. HE'S AT
a house in Sarvis Park.

What? Sarvis Park, that's a long goddamn walk.

Is he at Sarvis Park?

Yeah, that's where he is.

Why didn't you tell us before?

He asked me not to tell.

So why are you telling now?

I guess, I figure it's gone on too long.

Sarvis Park. What is it he's doing there?

He's with some friends.

Which friends?

I don't know.

You do know.

I don't know.

Have you been to Sarvis Park?

Yeah, sure.

So where is it in Sarvis Park?

It's by the water thing—the tall water thing.

Aqueduct?

Yeah, by the aqueduct. It's a big brick building, right next to it. I've been there a ton of times. We can go there. I'll show you.

Carson and Chester looked at each other. They stood.

You better start thinking about your own hide, kid.

He sounded almost sorry to have to say it.

What is it? What is it?

There's no aqueduct in Sarvis Park.

ANOTHER WAY OF LOOKING AT IT WOULD BE THAT A boy had been dragged out of his house, that a boy had been dragged up and down the town, that a boy had been dragged into this building and that building, and threatened and spoken to roughly, and that through it all he had just spouted nonsense like a pull toy. No matter how he was dragged, no matter where he was taken, his mouth went on mumbling anything at all. What do you do with such a boy? An embroiderer like that will just keep on embroidering. First he says to go to this avenue and then to that avenue to this boulevard and then to that. How can a boy be made to be serious when the heart of being a boy is irreverence and disrespect? How do you trick the answer out of him? Or is it just patience? Is patience a trick?

TO A BOY EVERYTHING IS FANTASY. AND THE FANTASY of a child is compelling. It is vivid and it doesn't feel very different from real life, except that it can't persist. At some point it shatters, and the thing that was there all along remains.

Maybe none of it was the way we've said, not exactly. Could it have been similar to that? Just similar? Maybe it was that people thought the boy knew something and they went about it nicely, just begging him to tell them. And maybe because he was afraid he thought of it that way, the way we've said: that he was hounded this way and that, beaten and hurt by thugs. Maybe he was just in a room, in a simple room, and people were being kind to him. The world we live in is unreasonable because however marvelous our fantasies become, real things are more marvelous still, and more frightening. Isn't it all just too terrible even to ponder?

MR. SPENCER SAT AT HIS DESK BENEATH A LARGE LITHO-
graph. The print showed the scene of a hanging. Underneath there was a banner that twisted through the crowd,
and the banner said in clear letters, THE DEATH OF THE
HERO LAMBERT MA. You would imagine such a picture
would be sentimental, but the details were all correct. The
body looked exactly as a hanged body should, and the expressions of the people in the crowd were quite correct.
These were people who had seen a hanging and now knew
both more and less about themselves.

The room was dark. All the things in it were of great expense. Harren Spencer had acquired them all, but he did
not enjoy them. What it was he enjoyed—that was not
something he had ever shared with anyone. What he did
share was his resentment. He resented being branded. He
resented having his thumb chopped off. He resented having to live in Row House. So he had plastic surgery on his
face and he wasn't branded anymore. He had a prosthetic
thumb, so his hand looked right. He paid the guards so no
one said anything ever. And he paid to make sure his son
wasn't branded either. That had been the plan all along. At
some point they would move out of Row House, and he
and his wife and son would live as pats. In the meantime,
he was a prosperous man.

He sat and looked at the carpet directly in front of his
desk. What was there, what was on the carpet was something that was of interest to him, but it was not something
he liked. There was a bench and a boy was sitting on it. He

had his head in his hands, and he was crying. The noise had been going on for some time.

Spencer's wife leaned against the window. Occasionally she would look out it and give them news about what she saw.

She'd say,

The helmets are pushing the crowd back into the barriers. Pretty soon the gas'll start. The brown gas, I think. Wouldn't you bet on it, the brown? Not the green?

Or,

Looks like this little bitch is even worse than the last. I heard half the stores on Weston are broken into. The hospital's full. God knows what will happen next.

Or,

Look at these people crawling out of the crowd on hands and knees. Could you imagine? On your hands and knees in a crowd?

She hated the Day of the Infanta. Or most of it she hated; she liked the part at the end. If things went badly and they chose against her, and the mannequin Infanta was thrown to the crowd, well, that was fun to watch. If that didn't quiet the crowd down, though—then they sometimes threw the actual Infanta down. Nobody really knew what to feel about that. It was the blood and bone of the festival itself—the heart of the whole thing. It was even especially senseless because the crowd was never calmer after they got the child in their grips. It sent it all off—and there would be riots and riots, and the guards would have to step in. Which way would it go? Of course they were safe in this house. Somehow rioters know—they should mostly destroy their own neighborhoods. And that's why the parade always ended back in the Lackal, the worst part of Row House.

She tapped the ends of her forefingers against one another very rapidly like type. She was nervous, and she talked when she was nervous. She was afraid, and when she was afraid she talked and talked, she talked just like her nervous self but more.

Where was her son? It buzzed through her head like the endless paths and shafts of never shot arrows. Her son. Ollie. She was his mother; of course she should think certain things. But it wasn't just her who thought them. Everyone agreed. Ollie didn't want much—he was quiet, sweet, had never had many friends. Until they found Eben to take him around. That had been his father's idea, and what an idea it was. Trust her boy to this older kid who leaves him somewhere in the city and comes back by himself like it didn't matter. She felt an anger rise in her, but it turned immediately on a wave of fear when her eyes passing along the wall found the clock. Another hour gone and Ollie was still not there. What good was it? Probably this idiot kid didn't even know anything.

LET'S LET THE LITTLE SHIT GO, SHE SAID.

She went and sat next to Eben.

He's a kid. She ruffled his hair. So we said he should watch Ollie. He's still a kid. How responsible can he be. Let him go.

Spencer watched her. He nodded.

You're right. If he knew anything, he'd have said it already.

Eben stayed sitting right where he was, stiff under the woman's hand.

If he knew anything, Spencer said, he'd have told us. A good kid would just tell what happened. It would have been the right thing to do, and he would have done it. Sometimes people who do the wrong thing, they're wandering along and they come to a point where there's a chance to go back, a chance to come clean. They've been on the wrong road so long, they don't think there's any prayer, any shot left, but all of a sudden there it is. It's good to be able to recognize that—to see when there's space to turn back, to be admitted back into the good life that was yours. Any clue might be enough to help find Ollie. Really anything might do, as long as it is a real thing, as long it is something that happened, somewhere you were, or someone you saw.

Eben's eyes were closed. What was he looking at, there inside his head?

THE REASON WE WANT TO KNOW WHERE OLLIE IS—IT'S because we love him. We're Ollie's family. You have a family. You know what it's like, said Ollie's mother.

Mr. Spencer shook his head slightly.

Well, our family is not exactly like yours, she amended. Your father's a piece of shit, and your mother's not much better. But you understand when I say we care about one another. We love one another, we take care of one another. You came along, last year, you came along and what did we do? We took you into our family. You became Ollie's great friend. Do you remember that? Do you remember how it was?

THE STREETS OUTSIDE THE HOUSE THAT HAD BEEN FULL of people—they were now run empty. Like water following itself wherever it goes, the crowd had pulled its tail after it. The parade had wound its way across the city and back, and the crowd in great anger had found some streets and surrounded them. It was always that way; at some point the float could go no farther, and that was the time for the judgment. Was it a holiday? It was a kind of organized civil collapse—and just then the moment was happening, in his beard the magistrate was stating his judgment of the Infanta, and of all she had done, and beneath a tarp they had readied the double, in case it went against her, and she herself, the Infanta, stood, completely consumed by the day, with no sense of what was happening or why or to whom.

The sun burned in the sky like a fever dream. It should have been gone already. The evening had come, but it was there at the horizon, burning on. Somehow it would not descend any further. Or was it just time stretching, as it does whenever the mind courses over the landscapes, leaping fences, climbing roofs? Our minds behold the burning sun, and the thousands of revelers, in their wild riot, the tableau from overhead, a catastrophe of arms and fists, and all of it on the hardness, the impossible hardness of cement, roads banged flat, poured flat so that they might be walked upon, a place made expressly to serve as the stage for our life's wreck. There was music, too, some song in the throat of every last singer, an anthem for those without anthems; it was the cry of the punished that there should be more—more punishment—more cruelty—more hate.

Always more, never less, that was the song, and it was sung with the whole of every heart.

But too there was a quiet note that came when the other went—and that note was a pale feather of a thing. It did little, it only named in order all that was, each thing one after another, a list of the world's contents, everything seen in its measure, every particle distinct.

And somewhere there was a rushing sound, as the entirety of creation shuttered back into one person's head, and then another's and then another's, a whole world for every raging member of the raging crowd, and for each one there was as much as for any other, and it was always too much—towns and roads and skies and rooms, stretching on into distances unfathomed—the world was always so much that the revelers had to flinch away, had to retire from feeling, and feel not what was before them but instead what they had felt, what they might feel.

EBEN LOOKED AT THE WOMAN BESIDE HIM. HE SHOOK
her hand off the back of his neck.

I'm not going to tell you because of your family or whatever you're saying, but because there isn't anything left but to tell it, so I will. Ollie's always making everyone do things, do this, do that. You know him one way. I know him another. He threatens everyone. He knows they're all afraid, well, Sat and me we stopped being afraid one day and that's when we decided we weren't going to put up with it anymore. We told him knock it off, and so what happened. He knocked it off, he treated us fine. That's his character. You have to make him do things. You got to know that too, I guess.

He leaned on his hands and looked at the spot where the front of the desk met the carpet. He didn't say anything for a while, and then he kept going.

Yesterday we went out to the ponds, the Sisters. If you've been there, you know, you leave Row West and go through the gate, they toss you, give you the shameshirt, whatever, you wear it and go out into the park, and you do it because you want to go swimming. The Sisters are right there, it's not far. They are the ponds, two ponds next to each other, one is like a tear, the other one is like a, I don't know, like a puzzle. I mean like a piece of a puzzle, jagged. They call the first one Lamp Lake, and the second Long Lake. Neither one is really a lake. I don't know why they call them that on maps. We just say the Sisters. Maybe you've been there.

So it's a hot day, and Ollie and me are in the street there, just out the window, and we think about going to the lake. Someone comes up with the idea, and we're trying to suss it out. Ollie says what's the difference, let's do it. So we go.

We get down to the lake, you know, it's Ollie and Sat and me, and then Porsino is there, and a few of his friends, and a bunch of girls they know, mostly a little older. Yesterday—maybe you remember—it was really bright, just bright as hell and hot. We get in—I mean, we've been doing it for years. Everyone goes there. The Sisters, you know, the ponds out by Row West.

The kids are just spread out around the lake. We usually have some people watch so we know if anyone comes. Sometimes the kids from another neighborhood will try to jump us, so you got to be ready. I mean, it happens out of nowhere, even out by the lake. But there were a lot of us this time, so, no worries.

He swallowed.

But the thing is—there's something special about the ponds, and all the kids know it. It's part of why we go. At one end, at one end of Lamp, sort of by this huge tree branch, there's a deep part, and it's real deep. We always dive there. There's a way you can do it, well, you go down as far as you can go, it's like half your breath to get there, and you find that the bottom of the pond turns, it turns, and if you fol-low it, if you go deep enough, there's an opening.

He looked around the room.

It's hard to believe, but the two ponds connect. I'm telling you they connect—under the ground. So we call the tunnel between them the divers' game. It's rough, by the time you get along it your eyes star up, I mean you're all dizzy and seeing lights, and then you have to go mad, you have to brutalize and just kick and kick and use it all and then you end up on the surface. If you're out of it, which I always am, then someone's there to pull you in.

Maybe ten people I know have done it, most people are chickenshit. I'm sure over the years other kids have. But I only know ten. Rin Lacau, Bat, Satler, me, Enid, Gan, Laranie, Stoub, Mavis, and Borman. It's a big deal if you do it. Some of them have only done it once. But you only have to do it once. No one will make you do it again.

Dive down. You just dive down and find the hole, then it starts. I mean you crawl. From one pond to the other. The divers' game. Always the same direction. No one goes the other way—it's a rule, because, I mean, what if two people did that at the same time?

He looked at Ollie's mother.

You'd meet in the middle, and there's no room to turn around. I'm always afraid of that, when I find the hole with my hands and pull myself in. What if someone's there? What if someone didn't know?

The part where, I know it's hard to see it, but, the part where you pull yourself into the hole is the worst. Because from there you just have to go on. You have to trust that the tunnel's the same. I don't know how many reasons there are that it could have changed, but you think of them when you're there, at the edge of the hole. Thing is, you can't wait very long there, because you need all your air to get through. So if you wait, then you have to come back up. Then the next time you go down you freeze a little more. You have a habit of sticking, you see? Like when you're going to jump off a rock, but you stop near the edge. It's harder the next time than the first time. Each time is harder if you stop.

Anyway, Ollie was too scared to do it. We teased him, we kept at him, play the divers' game. Don't you know the divers' game. He's kind of smaller, of course, and a shit swimmer. But there's a small kid who did it, Gan, he was smaller than Ollie, a lot smaller.

We'd talk about it, about the roots that you feel as you pass along, and which trees they must be a part of, and he was always left out, and the more he was left out, the more we would talk about it. We said it was the whole world, better than anything, just crawling along there. He wanted to know so badly, I could tell.

I said to him, there's a light down there. When you're halfway through, there's a rock that lets off light. It's silver colored and so pretty you could cry. You want to just stay there in the silver light, but you have to keep going.

Satler said he loved that light. He said he thought about it all the time, even when he was doing other things. There was nothing else to think about, nothing as good.

I said you expect it to be dark, and it is, but then you feel your way, and the glimmer is there, the glowing, and it is almost warm, like a dream.

Ollie asked why I never talked about the light before. I always said it was dark.

Satler said it isn't really exactly like a light. I agreed. It is very dark. But the light, when you see it . . .

THAT DAY THERE'S THIS GIRL THERE, LARANIE, AND
she's a good diver, I mean, she's better than me, for sure,
and she just lays into Ollie. She hates him. Always calls
him a pat. Spits on him. She's mean. She knows the divers'
game better than anybody. She does it just for kicks. She'll
get there and dive down, go through, first thing, without
even building herself up. I can't do that.

But she hates Ollie. Did I say that? She gets a couple others
to join in, so he's outnumbered and she's just ragging on
him, and he's sitting there on the bank looking down in the
water like there's something there to see. I couldn't even tell
maybe he was crying.

Some reason this time it's too much. So he clenches his face
and he tries, just like that, he dives down, and then a minute passes, another minute, and then he comes up and he's
coughing and coughing. He says it's too far. Everyone just
laughs at him. Suddenly he's the fuckup who can't make it
to the divers' game, let alone cross it. I mean, even kids
who haven't done it are laughing at him, probably so no
one thinks to turn it on them. That's how it works.

He's snuffling around there at the edge, maybe trying to
climb out, maybe just being busy hoping it will stop.

But she says to him, your dad's a big man, everyone knows
him. But you're not your father's son, you're nobody if you
can't find your way through the divers' game. And suddenly it does look a lot like he's crying—I don't know, it's

hard to tell in the water, but he tells her to screw herself. He takes a deep breath and he goes down again, and we're waiting and waiting for him to pop back up. One of the girls is counting out loud. Other girls join her. You hear their voices, like, happy and also just full of spite. They're counting and counting. Finally they just stop. Somehow they all want to stop counting at the same time, except one, and you hear her voice counting on, and then even she can't take it, she stops, and it's really quiet. Just the sound of water, maybe some machines in the distance.

No one thought he'd go through with it. Maybe he made it. It occurs to us. So half of us, we run across the grass to the other pond, and we're looking there to see will he come up. But he isn't there. We're looking real close. Where is he? He isn't in the one pond; he isn't in the other. Somehow no one wants to go in the water.

And then we get the feeling, all of us at once, that we better be far away. If you don't know what that's like, if you haven't been in a situation, I can't say, but your skin gets tight on your face, tight and cold, and all of a sudden you can think really clear. You can see how things are going, where they're going, and then everything is fast like sped-up film. No one looks at each other. No one talks. We all just walk away. It's like rushing, like hard wind rushing at you, and there aren't any thoughts in your head, just your legs running under you.

Then you're back in the street by your house and you want to pretend things are the same. You and everyone else, you all just make things the same, you want to try and say what you can say to have them be . . . to have them be that way, the way they were, the same. If there was something for anyone to know back where we were, well, no one knew it. No one looked, no one dove down and found it out, so it is hard to say anything even happened. Ollie could have slipped out of the water anywhere along the edge of the pond and just walked away. He could just be playing a trick on us. It would be like him, don't you think? You know him. You know how he is. It's the kind of thing he would do.

Letter

How many years did you spend
writing your death letter?

I t is eight in the morning. The sun rose and now stands over the house. I am sitting in the workroom—your workroom—a place I have always hated. I don't know how to tell you what it is—the place I've come to. I am trying. There is a joke you used to love to say—when we first met—you would say, *If you ever plan to leave, write me a letter. Don't tell me in person. I'm too weak to hear such things.* Well, now I am writing you a letter. I hope you will remember the joke and smile, though it might take years.

I'm sitting at this desk, and everything is inert. The chair is inert. The walls are inert. I'm helpless. I don't even know what I mean to say or how to begin. Alan, I was walking by the Gasklos buildings. I had left you here asleep at the house, and I went walking. It was early and still mostly dark. I went the way I always go, past all the shuttered shops, and then away by the dividing wall, then down to the Gasklos buildings. There's that corner there, where one of the buildings reaches out to the path, and you can't see what's ahead. I always think, I wonder what's on the other side, and then you get to the corner, and there's nothing there. There's never anything there. Alan, I didn't expect it. All my expecting led me in that moment to not be expecting anything, despite feeling expectation. I had grown used to my expectation, and then I came to the corner, and there was someone there. That part of my walk is solitary. At that hour there's never anyone, not on the walk, not in the street. He loomed out of nowhere. I don't know what he meant by it. He seemed large to me. He saw me, he spoke to me, he came toward where I was. It was only a few feet. I froze completely. If I was holding anything, I dropped it. He was speaking, but I didn't understand him. The light there is poor, and it seemed like something I had heard of. I had the feeling I was in the midst of something I'd been warned about. This is how it begins, they say, describing the very scene I was in, and it ends with you wretched and raped. I looked at him as he came and I saw his face clearly, totally, I've never seen a face like that, not yours not mine. That seemed a proof of something, of some destruction to come; why else would it be so easy to see him, to see his face in this detail—like he was claiming me, and that claim was that I would never, could never forget him. It felt like falling through a floor.

THE BELL JUST RANG—SOMEONE AT THE DOOR. IT wouldn't be you. I feel that in this moment I am so completely alone—alone from others and from myself—that for once I can feel close to you. For years we move toward each other and away. Sometimes I love you, sometimes not, sometimes I know you, sometimes not. Sometimes I love the one I know, sometimes I love the one I don't know. There have been times I wished you gone. That's what it is to live with someone. This moment I feel so close to you. That's why I can cry to myself and find this joke so funny: that I should write you this way. I think of the moment you find it. You'll enter the room, you'll see me there—not waiting, not not-waiting, not doing anything, lacking what I've always been, but missing nothing. Isn't that the confusion of death? The body is there, and it seems to the eye—nothing is wrong with it. Why should it not be inhabited by the one I love? It is not inhabited by the one you love. She has left it. Not to go anywhere—for all she was was that, that wretched pile of cells. She has given up what animation was hers, her life. Alan, I am so sorry. For you and for all your hopes. This small person I am has ruined them.

I THINK OF HOW I COULD HAVE RISEN THIS MORNING and gone a different way. Of course—that path, that way is the way I always go. But there have been times when I went a different way—and if I had, then in this moment when you sit reading my letter, my body beside you, your face contorted in some impossible cry or laugh, then in that moment I would be there with you talking. We would be talking in the garden, or standing in the hall, saying anything, nothing, anything. I feel even had I failed to turn the light switch on my first attempt. Had I, upon waking, groped a moment with the light switch, it would all be different. Standing in the pale light, dressing a quarter second late, I would be a saved woman. That gap would have stood complete, and complete it would have been my savior. But, Alan, I found the light switch on my first try. I dressed as quickly as I could. I rushed off to my appointment not knowing I had an appointment—still I went toward it like a woman driven.

I AM NOT YOUR DARLING—NO ONE IS ANYONE'S DAR-
ling really. We wear buckets on our heads and scream
ceaselessly like lunatics—this is an accurate picture of life's
maraud. But darling, I was standing on the path and instead of me standing there what stood there was some sem-
blance of me that contained all the training I have ever
been given. All that was horrible that was given to me was
present in me then, and there was no room left for anyone
I know or anyone you know, anyone you might have seen
in me. That man stood over me in the near darkness and
I quailed, and in quailing I leapt into a person I am not. I
remembered all the training I had been given. And what I
did was nothing I know, though I know it now.

Do you remember those classes? Have I told you how I
hated them? I was just a girl. I practiced and practiced with
the practice-gas, we all did. It was a game. Every day in
school to practice. You'd stand in the painted circle and
someone would try to get to you, and before they did you'd
put on your mask, pull out the canister, and pop the lid.
My school kept ratings, lists, rankings, who could do it
well, who needed improvement. I was a failure. The others could always get to me; I never pulled the lid in time.
Don't you see, the teacher would say, they will take your
mask and they will rip you into bits. This canister is your
life. Don't you see? I didn't see. My parents were called to
the school. Your daughter cannot protect herself. She must
have extra training, or she will be in danger whenever she
leaves the house.

I was dragged home in shame. My privileges were taken away. I was sent to a special program at great expense. There we took pains to learn every motion of that murderous routine. I hated it and I hated it and I learned to do it well. Who would have thought, said my instructor, that you're the same little reject who came here ten days ago.

I HAVE BEEN GIVEN MY WHOLE LIFE, AS YOU KNOW, TO thoughts of death—not always my own death—but to death thoughts. Somehow I have pictured myself in my final moments by a river, or holding a cup of tea, holding a cup of tea and sitting in a body so wrinkled and changed that no one I know would know me. That was how I pictured it. I felt it lay there, in those details. But right now I am sick all through my body and I want no tea. I made no tea. I am writing this letter on the desk you use for your pointless—you would describe them that way—writings. They are all of a piece, this writing, that writing, all writing: pointless. Yet we do it. Even in this I am a coward. I want to say something. I sit to write it. I fail to say it. I fail to say it. I fail to say it. I fail to say it.

I'll say it now. He was coming toward me on the path, and I found that I had put my gas mask on. I found I had in my hand the canister. I felt a swelling as painful as delight run through me, and I opened the canister, I tore off the lid. It was like a film. He tried to backpedal, but the gas moves through the air so rapidly, it reached him in a second and he was off his feet. Then I, recoiling, stopped. I went toward him. His falling down made me feel at once that he was a person—I went toward him and he was crawling out of the gas, clawing at the ground, trying to get away, making the most awful sounds you've ever heard. My sympathy twisted then. What if I had done the wrong thing. Had I done the wrong thing? I took his feet in both my hands and pulled him back into the gas—not because I wanted him dead but because I did not want to be confronted by him for having done to him what I did. Rather that he was dead than that. I pulled him back in, and he resisted like a child. I don't know if I was crying. I held his feet and watched him thrash. This was a grown man trembling like a laundry line, calling and calling with something like a voice. Was I crying? I don't think I was crying. I am not crying now.

WHAT I HAVE TO TELL YOU IS THAT THERE IS SOMETHING surprising I have found and what it is is this—what I have done to this man I absorbed completely. I did not run away. I did not go for help. I did not frame it comfortably in my head. I absorbed it wordlessly—absorbed all of him into me. I stood there on the path and felt what he was, what I was, what had happened, and I grew into something different than I had been. There is a permanent sickness in my stomach. It is a revulsion and it is a disgust, and it is a disgust at who I am and have been—who you are— who we are together—who everyone together becomes in this day and age out on the pavement. Perhaps there are arrangements—other arrangements of men and women that I could be a part of—but my own action showing me to be so perfect a part of this horrific society in fact demonstrates to me the exact nature of this society. In this I have my total knowledge, and I want no part of it. We are maintained by a violence so complete, it is like air. And because of that, I would rather die than anything, rather die than be alive. I'm sorry.

THERE IS A FEELING THAT WE ARE THINGS IN COMMON not alone. That I am myself in terms of you, and you you in terms of others. Together we make a world and go on in this sea of days and months. In this picture no one is their own—everyone is everyone else's; our bodies are the possession of our society. We might own things but never ourselves. Yet I think there is a different duty.

I see it differently—let me say, we never live but by taking resources that might have gone to another. We are hungry; our greed knows no bounds, and in the course of a life we consume what we must to proceed. We think that fair. Well, I believe, this being true, that a person who does not like life, who does not enjoy life, who enjoys, likes it no longer, has a duty to stop at once this feeding that takes resources from another's mouth. There can be no argument in favor of continuing a life devoid of caring, most especially not when it precludes the possibility of other delighted lives that might have been.

So you see I have thought about this. I sit here thinking about this. I am sick all through my body. I know you think it wrong to take one's life. I know most especially you will think it wrong of me to take my life and in doing so to ruin or alter what you can expect from yours. But my dear—this thing that happened, in happening it ruined me. It ruined anything I might give you. I am better gone and better gone sooner.

YOU TOLD ME A STORY WHEN WE FIRST MET AND YOU would walk with me to the university. You said that the girl you knew before you knew me—who you lay with and who went around on your arm—you said she was struck by a train. She was drunk. People were drinking, friends of yours, and she with them, and they drank enough that they thought it funny to stand on the train rails by a tunnel. But in their confusion they expected the train from one direction—it came from the other. Most of your friends jumped away, all of them, I think, except her. She did not jump away. You told me this. She was crushed completely and with her the first version of yourself that you had presented to the world. You told me this, told me her name, showed me her picture. I felt how you loved her, and also how you loved who you had been then—someone you could no longer reach. You said you experienced a cavity when thinking of her. So completely had she been killed that you could not remember the sound of her voice. To me it was remarkable. I loved you—and wanted all of you. I felt somehow I could be for you both myself and this girl, never mind that I knew nothing about her. I drew her in my head and grew to be her in part, and I did it for you. Sometimes when we were together and I would speak unexpectedly, act unexpectedly, and you reacted with shock, that was her in me, her voice in my mouth, her hand on my shoulder.

Why do I say this now? Well, I wonder—if she in her death made a gap the size of her life and you could see nothing but the gap, not her but the lack of her, I wonder, will my death make for you a widest gap, an incommensurable space, so that the effort of your life hereafter is just to live, to live on beside it? And will you feel when I die that it is not just me but also this girl, that I die, and that she dies for a second time, this person I tried to be for you, this attempt of mine in all the weakness of my heart to bring to you a self you thought you'd lost?

THIS DISGUST IN MY STOMACH IS A KIND OF PICTURE, and in it I feel myself compelled to wonder—what this man was going to do. Where was he going and why? Who was he going to see? Who is there that loved him? Even now they are learning that he is dead. That news is traveling on an intricate map—the measure of which is the exact dimension of his life. The lack of his life in that way fills his life—and those who know him cannot know why.

OR PERHAPS THEY DO KNOW WHY. MY REVULSION AT this place of our lives—this society of which we are a part—seems not to immediately admit an obvious truth: the people who are ground to bits by our horrific thought-lessness, selfishness, greed, though they may not know in each case why it has happened, they do not need to know. These things have happened so often that it becomes clear: a man like this did not die because of what he did but because of what he was. We are the ones who have the privilege of having things happen to us because of what we do. Not everyone is so lucky.

LET ME DESCRIBE FOR YOU WHAT I SEE WHEN I CLOSE my eyes. There is grass and a stretch of dirt. The dirt lies flat the way ground is supposed to. Something about it harms me. Its flatness is like a voice saying, look on, look on. Beside it there is the corner of a building. There are arms too, and legs. Arms, legs, a torso, shoulders, a face, hands, a face, and these are at the center of my vision. What else could I be looking at, wherever I might go? The face is bent, pulled in and out as though suddenly starved and gorged, and it gapes at me. The eyes are bulbs. This is the body of a man, this is a man about fifty, it is his body, and I look at his eyes, I kneel over him, and my skirt is touching him, I am touching him, I kneel and look at his eyes, but I can no longer tell their color. The gas does that. His shirt is coarse and blotched. I touch it as I crouch on him. I have never touched such clothing before, never crouched over someone in a street. Touching him shames me, for I am shamed by it, and I see now I should not be but am, which is my shame. I see there on the ground what he was carrying. A small valise. It has fallen open and I see what's there. A notebook, an apple, reading glasses repaired with a rubber band. All this I saw when I crouched there, and I see it now, and it shames me.

NOW I AM LOOKING AT A PICTURE ON YOUR DESK. IT IS a cottage on a hill. You said once to me the name of the person who lived there, some minister. You said he retired and fled the city at the height of his fame. He was a pointless person like all the other pointless people. But he did escape. I look at this picture and feel, I too am finding my nature in this flight.

HAVING SEEN THE BODY OF THIS MAN WRENCH ITSELF into garbage, I know what it is that awaits me on the floor of our house. I sit here writing, and as I sit you move toward me through space. I sit, I write, you come to the door of our house. I set down the pen, I take up the canister. You unlock the door, you enter our house. I open the canister, I breathe in and am caught up entirely. I cough, breathe, cough, breathe deeper, and, racked by coughing, fall. At the bottom of the stairs you hear a crash. You climb the stairs. Some filament of colored gas emerges from beneath the door, and this is my banner. This is what you first see. These are the tidings you have of me, and in them is everything you need to know, this whole letter in that sight. Meanwhile in the room I am curling desperately, wanting to beat my head against a curb to get the gas out. At the last worst moment it is done and the room is empty but for you wearing a gas mask and standing in the doorway. What is it you stand over? Something that was me just a moment before. It is a piece of theater we will have, this final tableau. I am so cold. I feel cold. I write cold. Can you hear it? I am so sorry. Alan, I am sorry. I wish I were not doing this to you.

IT ALWAYS SEEMED TO ME THAT THERE WOULD BE SOME warning—that I would have, at the least, a month to live before I would die. Thinking that, I felt that death could likely never reach me because my everyday life would need to be stopped by this warning—at that moment I would change, be someone else (the person so warned). In a way, then, my everyday self would never die because she would not be the one living the final month. In clinging to the everyday life, therefore, I felt I could avoid death because everyday life, to my mind, is a place to which death never comes.

I was wrong. In fact, the opposite is true. Everyday life is the province of death. It is where all dying takes place—for the extraordinary lands we imagine simply do not exist. There is only the ordinary. It is what we inhabit, and when death comes to find us it is there that he looks.

Looking over this account, I think I have said it badly. I was, it is true, out early in the streets. I was by the factories. The way the trees stand there so impassively—I have always felt a ready calmness that sends me on through the day. But he was there, this man, my terrible opponent, and I came upon him so suddenly.

I wonder, even, could he have come there for the same reason as me? To see the trees? I am so oblivious. Could it be that we two had been in that place together, morning after morning, perhaps for years, until one day I turned on him and killed him? Perhaps it is even likely. Why else would he have come toward me except to speak, to share something—a thought, something. This morning it was especially clear, the thin etch of the trees, and perhaps he felt what I felt in it and wanted to say so, to bridge this pathetic buffer that keeps one mind from feeling the presence of another.

If it is so, it would explain the way his hands outstretched—as if in supplication. When I see it now it seems clear: I killed him for being like me. What kind of suicide is it to kill in the world what you find in yourself?

A PERSON CAN DO WHAT THEY LIKE. THEY MAY STAY where they are. They may walk on some distance, may never return. I did not need to stay with him when he was dead because my killing of him was a non-act. It would not be felt by others whose feelings matter. It would not be felt by anyone I know. It was a non-act. I should not have felt it. It was not necessary to stay because staying would be dwelling on something common. But for me it wasn't common. Somehow I felt in this wretch a mirror of me. Anyway I did not stay but came straight home. Looking neither right nor left, I returned to the house. I drank a glass of water, and I went up to the room I am now in. I shut the door. This is the last room I will see. No other room is necessary for me. Let all the rest collapse in a breath.

LAST.

I forgot to say—I'm sorry—this last.

Please destroy all my things—all my clothes and my papers, the things people gave me that I kept. Please destroy them. I don't like thinking of such things staying on.

And when you tell people what happened just say, she had an accident. Talk about the woman you loved and say— oh, she was fine, yes, just fine, but then she had an accident. What happened to her was awful it's true, but beyond control, anyone could do it, could have it happen—to fall in a hole in the brain and know there is no way out. There isn't always a way out. Why, it happened to my mother and my aunt, and to her grandfather. It is a likely thing, you can say that, it was always likely, and you were ready for it.

Were you ready for it?

I know that you cannot understand me. But imagine it this way. Imagine I had killed an actual person, someone like you or me. Imagine I had done that, had seen another person in the light of day, and had killed them with no thought for their existence, responsibilities, loves, dreams. In doing that, you could guess I would have betrayed our life. I would have forfeited your affection. You could, seeing that, see that I was no one you knew. For me to be a figure of violence—I know I would stand against everything you believe in—your pacificism, your kindness, love, honor, learning.

What is it to kill a person? Something more than speaking out loud, and something less than being born. Something like knowledge, yet less, a knowledge that leaves you with less. In place of my life I have now only the impression of a graceful body, this man's body, as graceful as bodies are, this body twisted, wrenched, sprawled, and wrecked. He woke this morning and saw out a window the light of the world and went to it, not knowing he was moving toward me.

I KNOW YOU CAN'T UNDERSTAND IT, BUT LET ME TELL you, I have come to believe that in killing this man I have done violence as it would be to anyone we know. There is no difference. I feel it in my body, am revolted by it. Either it is wrong to think violence is only same against same or it is wrong to feel that they are not the same. I don't care which it is; I am certain one is true. This is the knowledge of my hands.

So you see, in taking my life I am taking a life that is more general than yours. My life is suddenly general, here at its end. The life I take from myself is the complement of that life drained out on this morning's path, fled out that man's ears, eyes, throat.

I am finding my character in fleeing. I arrive then in these last moments and depart again as a stranger to you.

your Margaret

ACKNOWLEDGMENTS

Jim Rutman,

Megan Lynch,

Catherine Lacey,

Catherine Ball,

Sasha Beilinson.